THE VERY RICH HOURS

Johns Hopkins: Poetry and Fiction
John T. Irwin, General Editor

The Very Rich Hours

JEAN MCGARRY

THE JOHNS HOPKINS UNIVERSITY PRESS

BALTIMORE AND LONDON

This book has been brought to publication with the generous assistance of the G. Harry Pouder Fund and the Albert Dowling Trust.

The Johns Hopkins University Press
701 West 40th Street
Baltimore, Maryland 21211
The Johns Hopkins Press Ltd., London

The paper used in this publication meets the minimum requirements of American National Standard for Information Sciences—Permanence of Paper for Printed Library Materials, ANSI Z39.48-1984. ∞

Some of the prose poems have been published previously, as follows: "Black Letter Vulgate" appeared in *The Antioch Review,* vol. 42, no. 1 (Winter 1984). "Dream Date" appeared in *Sulfur* 12, vol. 4, no. 2 (1985). "I Meet the Family and Show My Mettle" appeared in *Oink!* 18 (1984). "The Workhouse" and "Solitaire" appeared in *Black Ice,* no. 1 (1984). "Seven Last Words" appeared in the *New Orleans Review,* vol. 11, no. 3/4 (1984).

Library of Congress Cataloging-in-Publication Data

McGarry, Jean.
  The very rich hours.

  (Johns Hopkins, poetry and fiction)
  I. Title. II. Series.
PS3563.C3636V47   1987   811'54   86-46290
ISBN 0-8018-3504-6 (alk. paper)

Every hour that goes by grows younger.

R. M. RILKE

CONTENTS

PROLOGUE

To a Catholic, the world is divided by a line into the above and
the below, yet held together by that same line. The medieval book
of hours called *Les Très riches Heures du duc de Berry* is so divided. In it are pictures of the duke and his castle, of his peasants
and his animals, his festivals and hobbies. Alongside the calm
seasons and days of the royal life are other lives: the sorrowful
life of Jesus and of His Virgin Mother, and the difficult lives of
the saints. No final line is drawn in this book between the holy
and the daily. Even in those pictures of Jesus in His agony, deep
in the background is the bluish ducal castle in twilit calm.

Les Très riches Heures is a complex book, both an art book
and a prayerbook, a simple calendar and a holy office for keeping
the hours of the monastic day with its eight parts: Matins, Lauds,
Prime, Terce, Sext, None, Vespers, and Compline.

This book is also called *The Very Rich Hours*. In it is the story
of a soul, or beginner, entering the world. Weaving in and out
of this story are ornamental prose pieces, sometimes with a holy
subject, and sometimes with a comic. The hours in the life of this
beginner might be seen to overflow their boundaries and to spill
into the space between the chapters, and to color those spaces.

An hour in a secular life might be said to be enriched solely
by its deposit in memory, even as memory stains the hour to come.

THE VERY RICH HOURS

BLACK-LETTER VULGATE

And glorious Jerome, he drove his pen across a sheet of foolscap, heavy as a stone, stone-heavy his written heart, where Christ had once kissed and drove his fierce lips through Jerome's woolen garment, red, it was red and his eyes were red. His heart was black where Christ had placed his lips and sealed off the young Jerome from the world, from space, from illiteracy, from incidentals, and made his path ready for writing, for conversion, for signing over and again the crisscross letters of the Latin Bible, its vulgar and red face.

Soon he was old, old Jerome, Hieronymo, and his hands hurt, one hurt for the other, and the one hurt as Christ had hurt his heart with lips. He was old, still writing if it—that unguent and painted script—could be called writing, he was still writing and the name of God had come up those numberless times, and still, even after all those times, his writing heart contracted like the old and blessed thing that it was, fly-blown and dry with years, except for this one moment when his own lips would form the name of God, just God, and the many names he had: Jehovah, because it begins with J, and the ones that didn't.

Jerome, and his hand curled around a stylo or quill with a loose white plume and the sky so blue outside his medallion of a window and now the dark Gothic winter night and its own harsh beauty, beauty of thorn and berry, bone and incense, the soft fat thighs of Jerome on his bench in the icy sun, the bright scraps of color from the stained window, on Jerome's soft shoulders, a dusty crease in his lap and the cold winter feet.

Sing, Jerome, the father said, sing when His name comes up so I can hear, I up in the belltower, or in the morning garden spilling peas for the birds, if there are birds, and the brilliant spring and aching winter of writing, the writing of His name and the sheen of your sweet voice.

Winter bells, summer bells, the long carving, dreaming, coiling of letters and His name still surprises me. It always seems different and I feel different, my arm tensing in its own relentless labor and fingers apt to tremble. In my long and rigid infancy, my fingers limp, the book was near me in my mother's heart or in the crook of her elbow where I lay and heard, and lay and looked with the aqueous gaze of earliness, and before knowing my task, or any task—although I don't think of it as that, only the occurrence and recurrence of the name and the time when I stop and begin again. The interval after the sun spots the page and ink, when I go down for the interval. It might be sleep or the narrow eating hall, and the close sound of priestly prayers, an infinity of repeated motions so large as to be of no importance, and His name escaping into the air.

And back here the greater clarity, the frozen, the spring, the autumn and the lovely determinate, the beautiful transcription, answering and calling out again to the pure space that is Him.

EFORE the wedding day there was a small party and she was driven to it. The driver was talking. "We wouldn't have known," she said, "except by accident you were getting married at all." It was early winter and dark. The social worker, Mary Mallon, a fat woman with big full dresses and small boots, a face that never moved but delicate hands that traced a script under all her toneless words, had these hands in leather gloves, very thin, and curled around the steering wheel of the brand-new car, green, with no radio and no heater because Mary Mallon, she said to Miss Kane, didn't need one, she was warm all the time. Miss Kane, who would keep her own name on some cards, but would, she explained to Mary who asked for the second time, be Mrs. Frazier to the landlord and the registry, was never warm.

Never happy either, and wasn't happy, always a little sick, headache, stomach ache, flu. With these, the days at work were easy; the ladies in the day room made hot tea and brought in remedies from home; they wrapped her in the work sweater that hung on the hook in the employees' dressing room; took her out to lunch and talked in a nice tone. She wasn't as sick as the patients. They had sicknesses in the brain and personality, and their bodies were filled with medicine, which made them move slowly in their paper slippers and talk slowly, unless they were raving, and drink a million cups of coffee until their hands shook. You could learn a lot here. The very sensitive—Mary Mallon had said at lunch to Mrs. Propp, a nurse and Mrs. Jenkins, social worker—Miss Kane. That meant not sensitive; it meant she talked to the patients, addicted, poor, dumb, withered, and crazy, using a highbrow word she had learned in college, rubbing it in, the difference between them, might as well be dead as live the way they did, all shut in or on the streets of this old mill town; and herself, commuting from Boston with Mary Mallon and fresh from a snooty girls' school.

She was getting married. And what does he do? That was what they wanted to know. He might go back to school; she told them about that. There was a question of which school; for what? She'd think of him in his little room with the low ceiling, dark and warm; or him at the kitchen table playing his guitar; sometimes he sang. He'd drink a cup of coffee or a beer and put the lit cigarette on top of the can. Then she'd get a look at the face asking the question, and forget the answer.

Every morning at 6:15, the radio alarm went off and always the same song: "one less bell to answer, one less egg to fry," a sad voice. She was held by him in the narrow bed or backed up against him, the bed piled with his coat and the extra blanket. He opened his arms when he heard the song. "He doesn't have a job." She didn't have to say this because they knew it already, and now were having this party to which, after picking up a bag of fresh donuts from the donut factory, she was being driven.

They sat in the small living room, some on the braided rug, some on the couch, one on the hassock; the husband stuck his head in the door, all bundled up, and they pointed to the bride; he waved. Everyone had already asked all the questions they could think of. "Tell me," Mrs. Jenkins said, lifting her plate and easing her legs under her, waiting a minute to swallow the square of chicken salad, "are you going on a honeymoon, or just back to Boston? That's where you live, right, Boston? Is that where he comes from?" Mary Mallon said he was from New Jersey, but he was living in Boston; she turned to Miss Kane, who had a square of potato at the end of her plastic fork, and her mouth open. It was just then that Mrs. D'Ambra, the hostess, came in with a trayful of cakes, all white, and some decorated with small silver balls. "Here," Mrs. D'Ambra knelt next to Miss Kane's hassock, "these are for you." She put the tray down on the floor and wrapped a girlish arm around Miss Kane. Everybody was happy, so nice this Mrs. D'Ambra was and so sad she was an invalid with a collapsed lung and kept home so many days when things at the hospital were so much better for her being there.

For the present, going-away present and wedding present, a wooden spice rack, and a few spices wrapped separately. Miss Kane, holding onto the rack with both hands, face all pink from two glasses of wine, said thanks and then made a remark; it was off-color, that was Mary Mallon's thought, and surprising, coming from where it did, but the girl didn't say another thing of interest the rest of the night, although the ladies were all gathered around her, the bride. Only Mary Mallon had stepped back a little; she was stacking dishes in Mrs. D'Ambra's dishwasher. The party was almost over. "I missed what you said in there," Mary Mallon said in a tone as they got into the cold car and Miss Kane sat down with the present and the wrapping. "You must have said something funny. Would you mind repeating it so I can hear? You know me, I love a joke." I said, Miss Kane replied. Oh, never mind. It wasn't funny really. I have no sense of humor.

Miss Kane wondered why she had said this.

4

"Oh yes you do," Mary Mallon came back in an alert tone, starting up her car and pumping the gas with her small foot. "I've," she looked into the rearview mirror and backed out the driveway, "noticed that you do. You just don't believe in sharing it with people. You're probably going to share some of that humor with him, though." Mary Mallon was out of the driveway, and put the car into first. "It'll be hard on him if you don't."

Miss Kane, shivering because the house hadn't been warm and she had several hours of built-up cold, knew the social worker needed to talk it out. If she didn't work out this insult from a little nothing of an art therapist, it would come back. Miss Kane didn't feel—even though she had made the joke, then refused to repeat it, so it was her fault—she had the backbone to get through the last few days before she left the hospital forever to get married, with Mary Mallon trying to get it out, so she let the fat woman talk: work herself up, with her loud laugh, and clear her account of every word and action since the girl started working at the hospital, scared and full of herself; give it back to her now that she had the chance, take her down a peg or two.

Miss Kane, distracted a moment from the sharp talk in the smoky air, while the first shopping mall went by on the left, all lit up under the cold night sky but closed now, was thinking that if Mary Mallon knew there weren't a lot of pegs to be brought down, she wouldn't think it was so worth her while. This made her laugh, and when Mary Mallon heard the laugh, she relaxed; she had talked enough.

The next day, not a work day, she woke up the second time, and no one was beside her. Where could everyone be? Her bed was piled with blankets and a bedspread, tightly tucked in to fall with a nice, flat weight. It was already a sunny day; the walls were orangey and all things heavily lit and evenly, just the one long person in the bed quiet. She had kicked him out. He got up, put on his blood-colored coat—maroon or purple-red—shook himself loose and went out, away, into the hideous cold night, Kenmore Square. He would go— she followed him with her glittery eye, unfeeling, a mineral—to some diner or deli, for coffee; next, write something on a paper, a rebuke. She remained in these quiet folds. She could hear, now that she was awake, the sounds of the two lady doctors, the roommates, making their breakfasts: $1\frac{1}{2}$ slices of English muffin thinly spread with creamed cheese and thinly spread with strawberry bruises, a solitary glass of tomato juice rimmed and streaked, some dried fruit. The other one, with a long hank of blonde hair all braided or knotted, made watery tea and floated a lemon in it, then stirred it, first one way, then the other way. On her plate, cold cottage cheese and a cut-up fruit with a bran muffin, cold and unbuttered, or a slice of wheat bread. These were the breakfasts Miss Kane adored: they were listed and relisted in the fashion magazines with or without a picture: 1/2 cup, 1 slice, 2 small, 4 oz., 16 tiny but judicious and chaste pellets of nutritional self-observation and judgment. Eat this, you machine of glory. Mary Mallon would be taking a selection from the bag of donuts: I eat a donut; eat this donut.

She did have a sense of humor; God had given it to her. She waited in bed until they left. They put the two piles of dishes in the sink and she washed these dishes. They said don't do it, but she did it anyway. She visited one bedroom then the other; everything was fine. A thin perfume was still there near the outside door, something from a pretty bottle with a gold cap: exalted, humid, porphyry. A long doll was on Jill's bed, a big baby doll from the old days with rosy cheeks and a tiny mouth, eyes that opened and clicked shut with little brushes for lashes. Miss Kane picked the baby doll up and carried it to the window, Boston, Massachusetts. The phone was starting to ring. "Hello, this is Rogers Broughton; is Alex there?" Was she? No. She could picture this one: a tall, a wonderful.

She put the doll back, looked into Alex's room. Everything was just so. Curtains, curtain rods, sewing basket, magazine basket, shelf of poetry and handicrafts, wicker chair and melancholy old rug, a child's rug, all ripped and snagged. She opened the closet to the dresses: day dresses and night dresses, afternoon dresses and woolly dresses, skirts and skirt hangers, boxes of polished shoes with names marked on the boxes: Dove-gray High-heeled Pumps. The names were written with magic marker and what she loved was to look at the name and imagine: Sordid Pink Pumps, Filthy Frightful T-straps, how beautiful: Dilapidated Pock-marked Pillow Slippers, the shoe: Monstrous Mackerels, Sullen Flats, Big Bone Oxfords. She was laughing, then pulled a box out to peek under the lid to where each shoe was rolled in its white paper, uncrushed, when the phone rang again, hello?

❧ This was a nice day, cold, but they walked across the bridge from Boston to Cambridge, freezing, and he held her hand in a glove and mitten. He didn't wear gloves, or hat, or scarf, or boots, just a cigarette. He liked things to hurt; he wasn't going to go out of his way to protect a flesh hanging from its head, or the head propped on a stick.

6

She noticed this; something wasn't right about it, but just keep your mouth shut, nobody wants to know your business. Her mouth was shut and his mouth was shut, and keep it that way.

❧ She was getting married, see. There were a lot of reasons. Here I am on a silver tray, or a tray of silverplate or tin, a princess. This had not gone over, or it had stopped going over. For a while it looked like she could get on a silver sled behind these beautiful doctors and, acting like them, a princess, a beautiful golden . . . They had come, her parents (parents—that neautralizes it) to paint her room golden. She wanted it. It looked so pretty in the paint can, golden or goldenrod (that changes it). All the paint was slapped on the walls; it was wonderful, stomach-turning. All this color and nothing to hide it. This is what happened. She could be golden or silver but when the color was painted on, it was hideous. It was no one's fault, they were saying as they got into their car to go home. I know, she said, I picked it myself, me. They were glad to get away; everything she did was like that. They had driven to Boston to see how great things were, doctors and apartment houses and a new job. They didn't understand the words she used, but they could hear that they were good ones, cost money to get them; and leaving, they could see it was just the same old person they used to know, who used to live with them. They recognized who it was right away.

It was a yellow world, but she had done it to herself. No one asked her to ride to work every day with Mary Mallon; there were other ways, and why did Mary Mallon pick her out, Annie Kane, to despise; there must be a reason, it doesn't come out of nothing even if the girl is so fat and bitter. Miss Kane laughed. I picked this, I won't deny it; I picked everything myself; I was in the princess groove but I got out of it and got in beside Mary Mallon and rode to the nut house, and called my parents, Al and Marie Kane, when I needed a decorator. Go ahead, she was whispering in her yellow room, wash your hands of me, I asked for it.

Don't be too smart, little girl, was what the yellow wall was saying. This was what the old house would say, it's true, but the new house was just as good. When you're this kind of person, fat—even if you aren't fat—small-minded, impulsive, and always wrong, the world hates it, and why shouldn't it?

So she was getting married; someone liked her. Did he like her? He wasn't getting all she was cracked up to be, and he was getting other things he didn't even know about, although just a quick look at these walls, a trip back home, and circle slowly through the doctors and he should have known. Yeah, but did he?

She had no friends or allies. They had all drifted, the new friends, to their own cities, nice cities, to begin a life. They deserved this: they worked for it, and they were made for it. No one had ever said: you, we have this thing for you, come and collect it. For me, she remembered, things had come as far as here: Boston, Massachusetts, and this was far. Her mother had driven her as far as the school, turned around, and drove back as fast as she could. Now she was in the place, still there, where her mother had left her.

She remembered how long it took to get here. How long? There were no shortcuts. They loaded the car with the things they knew she had to bring, and they knew because they had studied the magazines and saw what these were and the college had sent a checklist. They read through the checklist and then they lost it, so toward the end it was guesswork, although anyone would know enough to bring sheets and pillowcases and a dictionary.

Where do you get a dictionary? her mother had asked when they were pushing the shopping cart through winter coats and winter suits at the Ann & Hope outlet, all one floor. Maybe they were against the wall with the pads and pencils. They were. How big a dictionary should we get? Miss Kane knew enough words already and there were too many she knew but didn't like to use except at school when she was forced to fill out a composition. She hated looking up words. Her mother was looking up a word: caramel, to see if it was there, or if it was spelled carmel like people around here said it. "Aren't you interested in this? How are you going to go to college if you're not interested?"

They picked up an orange Webster's college dictionary, $4.99, a paperback, then they wheeled the cart to sportswear, where the mother saw the word jerkin on a sign, burgundy heather wool-blend, and looked it up. "See, I'm getting a lot of use out of this. I should have bought myself one. Why don't you look up a word? You'd like it if you'd just try."

Her mother loved the idea of college but she couldn't visualize what you did there all the livelong day. "You steady," her grandmother, who also loved the idea, said, when they were discussing it and the old lady was coming up the cellar stairs with a load of laundry to butt in on what was a private conversation, like she always did. Her mother thought the grandmother was making too much of that because she loved to read and would lie on her bed with an

Ellery Queen and the transistor radio playing "beautiful music" all afternoon on weekends when the soap operas weren't on, the stories, as her grandmother called them. She loved a book just like Annie did. She doesn't read the same books you do, the mother tried to tell her mother, but the grandmother knew a book was a book and her own daughter didn't like any books, too tedious. You get it from her, the mother had told Annie; you don't get it from me, or him— he hates books. Annie's father, Al Kane, hated books; so did her brother, Jimmy Kane. That's why there were no books in the house except for the grandmother's books, and she liked to keep all her books in her own room where no one could steal them, or see them and criticize.

There were a few children's books in the cellar: the *Golden Encyclopedia*, which you could get in the supermarket, $.99 for the first volume, *Aardvark to Bombardier*, then $1.99 for each volume to come, and every week a new one appeared on the shelf: *B* was yellow, *C* was green, *D* was orchid. What color is this? she had asked her mother, who was reading her shopping list, and she said orchid. "I don't have enough with me this week for that one," she said, and Annie put it back on the shelf, next to the yellow, green, and white. Can we get it next week? "I don't know; don't pester me with it now." The next week, it was gone, it had sold out—the orchid one—and they missed it; they missed a few others, but after a while, the colors started repeating. "You've got enough of them already; you haven't read them all yet, I know you haven't," Mrs. Kane told her whiny daughter, carrying two volumes, *T* and *F,* of the encyclopedia and trying to get them into the shopping cart already filled: cornflakes, oleo, potatoes, roast beef, peas. "Why don't you read it here, instead of jawing at me?" she said. "Go on, read it. Look up a word."

They had a few hardcover books from the Book-of-the-Month Club which Uncle Ed belonged to and sometimes passed on a book he finished but didn't want to keep; in the bookcase was a nice set of red books about World War II, no color pictures, but a few maps, and also these books from Uncle Ed; some of them were good, some of them she didn't understand. There were also a few magazines in the magazine rack, *Look* and *Life,* all ripped and ugly, a copy of *Holiday* magazine and, for a while, one of *Esquire,* from Uncle Tom, who sometimes brought magazines by. She looked through them, enjoyed looking at the dirty jokes about ladies in *Esquire,* until her mother caught her looking and told the father to discard these magazines that were trashy and not for children.

There were schoolbooks, but the nuns didn't like the schoolbooks to go home and be abused, even if they were covered with brown paper and stamped "SCHOOL PROPERTY"; but there was an old spelling book in the basement; *Our Little Speller, Grade Two,* and a hymnbook with old-fashioned pictures of beautiful trees, gingerbread houses, and water babies.

After a while, they didn't get spelling books in school anymore; all they got were thin sheets of pink paper with thousands of tiny words on them, hard words: assassinate, interrupt, peninsula, license. She knew all these from spelling bees and from using the same sheet for three years until she knew the order of the words, too, and could rattle off whole columns. "Wait for me to ask you," her mother would say. "Don't put words in my mouth. If you're so smart, why don't you go ask yourself in your own room?"

With the dictionary, they bought a purple wool suit, a blue jumper and a red corduroy dress, a gold pin, two pairs of stockings and a new black pocketbook, a package of pens, and batteries for a radio. This was one shopping trip to use the money Annie had made that summer; there was another: shoes, towels, bedspreads and a pair of tan slacks—although you couldn't wear slacks on the campus—and it was time to pack the car and go.

❧ It was snowing—was that snow? Sometimes things fell from the sky in Boston that weren't snow; but it was cold enough for snow today, so those things could be snow. It was already afternoon and the student doctors would be coming home in their cars to change their clothes neatly and do some shopping in their street clothes, or go out for a drink with a date, but come back home in one hour to study for the rest of the night, or cry on the phone to their mothers about their aches and pains and the mean resident on the surgical rotation. Annie Kane had seen their books and instruments and loved watching Jill or Alex standing in front of the bathroom mirror, twisting a rubber band around her hair and then a grosgrain ribbon, or making a bun that was pretty with bobby pins and invisible barrettes and looked simple and neat over the white jacket with the black tubes in the pocket, and the leather case full of small hammers and silver tappers and rubber eggs. Their books—some of them just books of tables and formulas; others were pictures of hideous diseases and openings on the skin and into the body: sores, cancers, ulcers, abscesses, cicatrices, abrasions, wounds, or things starting in the body and moving out—covered all parts of the body in a thorough and sickening way. They were proud of working in this field and becoming smart in it, even though it was hard every day, and annihilating—or this was how it sounded when they would go on rounds with the main doctor: Annie could picture them, tall men and tall women in a tight pack following a single mean doctor from bed to bed while he yanked the sheet off a skinny patient, an old man or a tiny girl, and pointed with a little stick (no, they don't do that; I know) at the bandage, and then pelted them with questions, and sometimes Alex—especially Alex—broke down under the pressure; but both girls were going to be psychiatrists and could forget everything they learned about blood and sores and pumping hearts. She had a psychiatrist, Annie Kane, and they knew this and no one was surprised. His name was Ralph R. Eagle, M.D., Ph.D. She liked him, but he was also the doctor of Jill, and had told her, Annie, not to bring him messages from his other patient ("Jill said to tell you"). "I'm your doctor," he said in his calm way, sitting in his leather chair with his pipe in the ashtray, "you don't have to deliver messages from other patients. You just tell me your own messages." This was such a nice thing to say and in such a tone that Miss Kane was silent the rest of the session, and Dr. Eagle silent, too: when she was silent, he was silent. This is how it worked.

Jill was jealous of Annie Kane's doctor; this is what Alex told her one day when they took the subway into Boston to shop and to have a muffin. "Buff doeskin western boots" with informal blue jeans, a white blouse with a ribbon around the neck and a plaid blazer, hair in a thick ponytail with a red grosgrain ribbon.

"Do you see," Alex had said in the subway; they were both standing and facing the dark window; "how thin my back is getting?" Annie Kane said yes, but she couldn't see through the jacket and stiff blouse. She had noticed Alex was eating one-third of the normal ladies' breakfast and rushing out of the house before dinner to go on a date with her new boyfriend, then coming back and closing the door of her room for the rest of the night—with him in there. Annie Kane could hear them listening to records and laughing. One night Jill came into Annie Kane's room, which she never did, and sat on the bed: "I can't work," she said, running her fingers quickly through her hair, "if they're going to be so inconsiderate. Why don't you tell them to quiet down; you need to sleep if you're going to get up so early in the morning." Jill got up to look at her hair in Annie Kane's mirror. "You wouldn't do it, though, would you? You don't care how noisy it gets around here. Well, *I* do and I'm not going to put up with it." Jill went back to her own room, but Miss Kane could hear her pacing in there and saying things in a loud whisper. Finally, the girl came flying out of her room with a storm coat and her books and slammed the front door. Alex ran, a minute later, to that door and opened it. "Anne," she said in a loud tone full of anger. "What?" "Will you come out here a minute?" Miss Kane got up from her unmade bed where she was trying to get a lacing back into a suede boot and it was hard because the holes were so small and the lacing end was all frayed. There was Alex in a day dress, candy-striped with long sleeves and T-strap pumps, with her arms folded: Annie saw the boy in the dark doorway of the bedroom with his bowtie; he waved, then closed the door. "I think we have a prob here," Alex said in the awful, cruel voice which Miss Kane was afraid of. She had used it on her one time before: "I don't want to hurt your feelings," she had said, standing in the doorway of the hideous gold bedroom, and then stepping in and sitting down on the bed, "but I've been noticing you skipping days of work and staying home." Miss Kane was embarrassed and turned her head away. She had been trying to arrange the hose of her hairdryer so it would fit in its case and not have to be put away in a big pile on the closet floor, but stacked like a little suitcase the way they did it and something on top of that nice and neat. She didn't want Alex to see how sloppy that closet was and the door flung open for anyone to see. Alex said she envied Annie a job like the job she had; they were hard to get, and the perfect kind of thing if she wanted to go to medical school and be a psychiatrist, but instead of making use of it and being patient the way Alex and Jill had told her when they first heard of the job and how ideal it was, Anne was irresponsible. "I didn't realize you were like that," she said, and now she saw the closet, but didn't seem to notice. "I don't think you can afford," she said, "to lose your job. I wouldn't want to see that happen." Miss Kane started to cry and Alex put an arm around her and told her she should talk about exactly these kinds of probs with Dr. Eagle, who would help her. Annie said she would and Alex told her that then—and if she went to work instead of staying home—things would be better and she'd be on her way and maybe even meet someone interesting. Alex gave Anne Kane a big smile. "Okay?"

"Where'd she go?" Alex said. "Did she tell you what was wrong, or did she just fly out of here in a rage?"

That was how Miss Kane knew that Jill and Alex—who graduated together and Jill went right on to medical school, Alex a year later, two of the five women in the whole school and a credit to their college; Annie knew; she was there and heard about it; and then roomed together, shared a nice flat in Brookline close to the medical school and the museum and other things—were having problems, or probs, as Alex called them. But it wasn't until the shopping trip to Cambridge that Annie Kane knew how bad things were, and it was all because of Dr. Eagle, that's what Alex said, "and I'm glad it's just the two of you and I have my own doctor, because I wouldn't put up with that one minute the way you do."

Alex and Annie Kane were sitting in the Pewter Pot; it was very warm and the top of the table was sticky. Miss Kane was eating her favorite blueberry muffin and brown mug of thin coffee; Alex was drinking tea with a cranberry muffin, but just picking around the edges of it. This was enjoyable, although Alex was looking very closely at her while she ate and her mouth was a little dry and things getting caught in the front teeth and her hand shaking when she lifted the full cup of coffee. "Do you see what I'm saying?" Miss Kane said yes, but she didn't see why it made Jill so mad that they were both patients of Dr. Eagle. They didn't go on the same day and they talked about different things: Annie Kane knew they did. Dr. Eagle was talking a lot about dreams and she was having more of them because he was talking about them and asking her to bring them in; they didn't talk about work or school or boyfriends which is what Alex said Jill talked about, "and me. She talks about me a lot," she said, touching the flat lemon with her finger, then putting the finger in her mouth.

Miss Kane was silent because she wanted Alex to talk more. "You see why she talks about me, don't you?" the girl said; now she was looking out the plate glass window into Harvard Square, those blue eyes like a baby's eyes all round and watery; Annie Kane couldn't see what she was looking at; maybe she was just staring. "Yes." "No, I don't think you do; you're so naïve." "You mean getting along at home and remembering to dry mop the living room floor, not sweep it?" Alex fixed the blue eyes on this face and laughed. "Do you really think that? She doesn't care about that. She doesn't notice you; she doesn't notice anyone but herself." Alex was looking out the window again, so Miss Kane took a bite of her muffin. "You don't see what's going on, do you? I'm surprised. You sound so smart some of the time and you're so analytical, but you're not that smart about people, and you're not smart at all about her." Miss Kane was listening. Alex reached in her small leather purse for a tissue. "Do I have to spell it out? She's a lesbian. And I don't have to tell you who's she's in love with, do I?" Alex blew her nose softly so no one would hear. She patted her nose. Miss Kane could see her face preparing something, but she could also see the girl scrutinizing just how this something was going to be taken in. Whatever it was she was going to say, she didn't say it.

Miss Kane didn't say anything either; she had to think if this was true. It didn't seem possible, but very interesting things had happened since she went away to college and she was never that shocked at a surprise like this; in fact, she liked it because it shifted the blame for everything off her and her ways, which she knew by now were not appealing and caused many probs at home and elsewhere, onto something else, something completely out of the blue.

Alex was smiling and sticking her lower lip out and her chin under it; Miss K. didn't like this look. "Well, I have shopping to do, if you're finished," she said. "Do you want to come with me?" Miss Kane, elated, said she did, and very little else was said. "Wouldn't you," Alex said, counting some change for the bill, "agree, now that you know—you live in the house, you see things—doesn't that explain a lot?" Annie Kane said it did, but she didn't know what. She thought about the possibility of it as they walked to a sweater store where Alex had ordered a rose-pink Fair Isle sweater with a lavender design around the collar, and then to a men's shop to buy a gift for Alex's father's birthday, then to the soap store and the bookstore until Alex had a big dark green shopping bag from J. Press, full of a J. Press shirt and other things; and a list of groceries to buy at Sage's—special groceries: tea and jelly, Pepperidge Farm cookies, cocktail olives and onions, crackers and sherry which, Alex said, would go into the picnic basket in her room for a light collation when Miles visited that evening. Now, she added, no one can complain about interruptions and inconveniences in our household. Alex went on to say that she would spell this out for Miss Intolerance, who was all too well known as someone who would filch other people's food even when it was specially marked. Jill would not like this. *Tant pis,* Alex said; she wasn't treating either Jill or Anne any worse than she'd treat herself, knowing how *she* would feel if there were cookies anywhere in the house not under lock and key.

Annie Kane, watching Alex move so swiftly up and down the narrow aisles finding the precise things she wanted, wondered if this new boyfriend, this Miles—no, it couldn't be, could it? "His name, although I doubt you know him—he's doing post-graduate work at the B-School and lives in Boston; he already has a degree in law and in I-don't-know-how-many-other-things—is Miles Kasendorf; he's Jewish." Alex was looking at her with the round eyes wide open but very focused. Anne Kane said no, she didn't know him; he just sounded familiar.

They got on the subway and the subway rushed them home so Alex could change into study clothes and shut her door for the afternoon. Jill was in the library on Saturdays, or home in New York, and Miss Kane, with nothing to do, decided to take an afternoon walk.

It was much too cold, but she stayed out for a long time. It was a surprise to hear Miles was back. She was walking through one of the fens looking at the bare trees; beyond them was the big white building of the museum. There was a new Chinese show in there, landscapes even drearier than this one. She was wondering if he might have seen her already and not said anything to Alex. But maybe he *did* say something and Alex was trying to hide it.

It wasn't that much of a surprise that he was back; it was more of a surprise to see him racing her way on his bike. She saw him before he got off the bike, pulled it up over the curb, and got on it again to ride over the frozen grass, then got off it again because it was too bumpy on the grass.

"Well, if it isn't," he was out of breath and could hardly talk, "Miss . . . Anna Marie . . . Kane. Good . . . afternoon, Ma'am."

He had on his usual topcoat and penny loafers; a jockey cap with belt in the back and wool scarf twirled around his neck whose wide stripes stood for a boys' school, Annie Kane still didn't know which one, one of them. He was grinning. "Remember me? I remember you.

"I knew you were here. I mean, I didn't know you were *here*, right here, I knew you were in there with them. I heard you one day and I thought, Cripes, there's Fanny Kane, what's she doing here? And here you are."

Annie Kane was smiling: she could feel her face all rigid and tight, and Miles looking at it with a strained expression. "You don't seem to remember me.

"I even know where your room is," he said. "They've got you in the back of the house, right?" Annie Kane laughed. It sounded like she was in the cellar with the roots and the rats.

"Where were you going?"

"There," pointing to the Museum of Fine Arts.

"Really?"

They were still standing there. "Is that Sung exhibit still on? I haven't seen that yet."

"I don't know. I'm not going to see that."

"Were you going there now?" He took his gloves off to look at his watch; it was the same watch, Annie Kane could see that, with a striped ribbon for a watchband. He was silent and he usually had so much to say.

"Do you mind if I join you? I have the time." He was reaching in his pocket for something. He took out a limp leather envelope and inside it was a small pipe which he tried to light in the middle of the freezing fens, but it wouldn't light. "Well, never mind. Shall we?"

He was just turning his bike, but she had already walked away — in the wrong direction—making a path of tight holes in the snow.

"Hey, Annie. Annie!"

❧ She was at work, 1:30 or a few minutes after, when she got the call. They had just come out of group therapy, or group, as they called it; a nurse, Mary Mallon, Anne Kane, and twelve patients sitting in a circle on metal chairs in a small room with cement block walls and turquoise blue linoleum. Marie Battiste was swearing and Joey Mahan had sunk into himself again, and hung his head until it touched his knees. He was forty-five years old, short and thin with a raggedy cardigan sweater he wore every day over a flannel shirt and bulky gray pants. Sometimes he had a lot to say and someone would have to quiet him down. It wasn't easy because the other patients would get involved too, and egg him on until he'd be in the middle of a long and not very funny—although Joey and Barry were choking with laughter: they were friends—monologue about growing up a little kid in North Andover and being an altar boy and a choir boy, a grocery boy and a Pfc. in the United States Army, 1947, 1948, 1949, then coming back to get a post at the old E. E. and L. B. Bloom Shoe Manufacturing on Main and Putney, closed down these many years, sweeping the factory floor from 5:30 P.M. to half-past nine, then begin again in the shoe outlet and the storage room until twelve, lock up, punch out, and there he would be, Joseph A. Mahan, in the middle of the night on Main Street and Main Street all closed up and dark, locked up and not a soul in sight, high and dry. So what'd ya do, Joey? Barry was saying, but someone else was saying Joey had talked enough and to give the other patients a chance. It was quiet a minute, then Joey started up again.

"What'd I do? Did you ask me what'd I do? What did I do?" He looked at Barry and Barry looked back. "I don't know what I did! There wasn't a goddamned thing to do!"

"There wasn't a goddamned thing to do," Barry echoed.

"There wasn't a goddamned, friggin'," Joey said, "thing to do, so I went home to my mother, stayed home." He was quiet a minute, then winked at Barry. "Unless I didn't go home to my mother. Then what'd I do? Ask me what'd I do?"

Barry was ready to ask, but Joey kept talking; he didn't wait for the question.

"What I did, since you ask, is have a few goddamned belts, or a tall one; two tall ones, half a dozen tall ones and a belt; what'd ya say, half a dozen and a belt or two, am I right?"

Barry was nodding furiously, but the room was quiet.

"Goddamn right, I'm right, Goddam fuckin' assholes!"

By then, Miss Mallon, whose face was red with irritation, had risen from her chair all in one movement using her feet and ankles, springing up so the whole bulk of her was steady on those small feet, and walked through the empty circle to advise Barry, cringing and trying to hide his head in his shoulders, to leave his seat, please, and take hers. Miss Mallon sat next to Joey. Joey was not looking at her; he was looking at Mrs. Peters, winking and nodding.

Miss Mallon took Joey's hand, half covered by the huge frayed arm of the sweater. She held his wrist with a finger and thumb, shaking it every few minutes. "I want," she said, "to say something truthful about Joseph Mahan, and I want you all to listen." Miss Kane could see, although she was new to group and new to the Center, what was coming. Joey Mahan's story was going to be retold in a different way. What the patients got here, as Mrs. Peters had told Miss Kane in her tiny office when Miss Kane had asked her if they could discuss one of *her* patients—schizy and on drugs, an outpatient mostly, although he was committed to the ward once every couple of weeks for an overnight; they hesitated to admit him, she had heard from someone else, because he brought his drugs with him and at least one of the other young patients would be hopped up too, and have to be confined. Eddie Foley was never confined. The quantity of tranquilizers they had to give him to keep him on the ward was dangerous, given the other things he was taking, so he was allowed to wander around and where he always wandered to was the art workshop where he could drip poster paints over cutout pictures from *Time* and *Life* and play his favorite record, "MacArthur Park," about the cake, on the little phonograph. The workshop doors were unlocked from 10 to 11:45 and from 2 to 4 and Eddie was there during those set times, a regular. Joey was a regular and so was Barry, but most of the other artists were teenagers, who liked records and paints and messy tables and floors. It was supposed to be messy, that's what they had told Miss Kane; it was the one place in the center where patients could do exactly what they wanted with no surveillance and no interference; it was where they could express their rage, Mrs. Peters told Anne Kane, so don't try to restrict their work. Let them do what they like; you're not here to be an art instructor—was something called Reality Therapy: no matter how crazy the patients were, no matter how hyper or depressed, how drugged or electrocuted (Miss Kane had seen the all-white room where they strapped them down), they were always told exactly what the world would demand of them if they were normal and they were to file this information in there with their delusions, and eventually the one would win out over the other, like it does, Mrs. Peters went on, in your life and my life. I see, Miss Kane had said. All the mills—shoe and textile—had shut down and underneath the problem of insanity, she figured, were other problems of unemployment and kids and mothers on drugs, and underneath that, the Irish pride, even in the crazy ones, that kept them from using food stamps in a store where anyone could see, or going down to the welfare in broad daylight, or to the hospital with a black eye or a broken arm when the son or husband, out of work too long and starting to frequent the barrooms and taps, taverns and saloons, clubs and packies, more per square inch than any place on earth—is that it? That's part of it, Mrs. Peters said grimly, and Miss Kane liked her for saying it. Mr. Mahan, Miss Mallon was saying, holding up the sleeve with the hand curled up inside, doesn't want to tell you, so I'll have to tell you who was at home those nights he didn't *go* home but had his belts and his tall ones. Who was at home, Joseph, with not enough food in the house and a sick child—Joe and Evelyn Mahan, Miss Mallon turned to the group to explain, had a mongoloid child and another child, isn't that right, Joey? with spina bifida, but doing a little better now, right Joey? going regularly to the handicap workshop. The other one died. The mother tried to take care of her at home, but—

Joey was crying into his other sleeve. "Stop blubbering, Joseph, and listen to me. We're all in trouble here and we have to begin by being honest with each other, don't we?" Miss Mallon looked up and around the circle at the other patients, eyes wide or popped,

18

those paying any attention at all; most were not. "Of course we do. Why else would we be here? You've got to face facts, Joseph Mahan. We're going to help you right now to do that, but first you have to be honest with yourself."

It was a terrible story. Joey Mahan, Miss Kane heard for the first time but it would come up again, had never had a job at Bloom's; he had never been in the army and might not have been a grocery boy, an altar boy, or a choir boy, but Mary Mallon was not going all the way back to destroy his lies and stories. She focused, as he was supposed to focus and they all were to focus, on being an adult and why he had never been one when it was time to be one, and neither had they.

After a while Anne Kane stopped listening. "He kill his kids?" she heard Marie Battiste ask Mrs. Peters. Mrs. Peters looked at Marie and everyone else looked at Marie because she didn't ordinarily say anything; she just swore. Mrs. Peters said no, Joey Mahan hadn't killed his kids through abuse of alcohol and mental illness. Plus, only one of his kids was dead, the retarded one, right, Joey? Barry piped up, but Joey didn't answer. After a while he got up from where he was sitting, pulled his sweater out of Mary Mallon's grip, and left the room. You could leave the room if you really had to—this was the rule—but you were supposed to stay till the end. No one said anything. Mary Mallon changed her place with Barry and Mrs. Peters cleared her throat. "Let's change the subject," she said.

Mrs. Peters, a beautiful woman, tall and red-haired with a slim body and carefully matched clothes, who ate a skimpy lunch of crackers and celery sticks in the cafeteria, avoiding the puddings and cakes, cookies and fresh pies baked by the cook, who used to own a bakery of his own in Lowell until he retired and went to work at the Haverhill Community Mental Health Center, and sometimes went to group because of problems with his wife and his daughter-in-law—he loved the center and would never leave it, he had told Miss Kane, no matter how old he got—was now talking to Ginny Cooper, a sixteen-year-old who came to the hospital when her mother couldn't get her to stop vacuuming her room. She vacuumed all night for three nights in a row, then the family brought her in. Now she was almost ready to go back and Mrs. Peters was getting her ready. The girl was carrying a volume of Anne Sexton's poems; she was rewriting all the lines to fit a rhyme in. Miss Kane was helping her. She had the volume on the floor next to her chair. The nurse had just given Ginny a list of things she could do during the day to fill up the time until she was well enough to go and finish sophomore year. The list was in short spurts: Annie Kane was sitting next to Ginny Cooper and she looked at it:

8:00 Rise.

8:15 Breakfast: 1 fruit, 1 carb, 1 protein, your selection. Consult mother.

8:30 Jumping jacks, knee bends, sit-ups; 5–10 min. Work on Anne Sexton.

8:45 Tidy room and bathroom.

9:00 Walk to the HCMHC.

9:15 Arrive and check in, take medication, hang coat, go into day room.

FROM 9:15 to 4 FOLLOW HCMHC DAY PLAN

4:00 Walk home.

4:15 *Help mother* with chores.

4:30 15 min. work on Anne Sexton.

4:45 Take a little walk, around the block or up to Reading Street and back.

5:00 Prepare dinner *with mother.*

5:30 Eat dinner.

6:00 Help with dishes.

6:15 Read two stories in the *Lowell Sun,* one on the front page, one on the women's page; cut them out and bring to the HCMHC following day.

6:30 Continued from above.

6:45 Choose clothing for next day; sew on buttons or iron, if needed.

7:00 Hand washing.

7:15 Poetry (Anne Sexton) at bedroom desk. *Listen to radio,* any station.

7:30 Watch television programs *with mother and father.*

9:00 Bathe, brush teeth, put on pajamas, hang or fold clothes.

9:15 Prayers and lights out.

It was a good list, and there was no gap in it for Ginny Cooper to get involved in a monotonous activity and keep going with it. Mrs. Peters had asked her to get an electric clock that would ring every fifteen minutes, just in case. The girl had a little color in her face and was talking more slowly. In order to talk, she had to drown out Marie who raised her voice to a screech every time little Ginny Cooper tried to talk. Mrs. Peters moved to sit next to Marie, and Marie took the nurse's hand. Every few minutes, Marie Battiste would kiss the hand front and back. Everyone liked Mrs. Peters, even the raving maniacs, but no one used that word. What they called them they got from the doctors and stuck with it even when the doctors moved on to a new one, and that was schizy; that's what poor Marie Battiste was, and that's what everyone else was too.

Time was up and Mrs. Peters had to walk Marie back to the ward. Anne Kane could still hear her from downstairs, where the main phone was—one of the aides had come to the art workshop at 1:35 to get Anne Kane for her call.

Annie Kane didn't get calls that often. Not that many people knew the number. "Hi, Anne?" It was a man's voice, and loud. "Is this Miss Anne Kane?" Annie said it was. "Well, hi, this is Miles. I had a lot of trouble getting you." One of the patients, Barry, coming out of the coffeeshop had missed the opening and bumped into the doorframe, spilling hot coffee onto his face and all over his green shirt. He was crying and the receptionist jumped up and pulled him by the hand back into the coffeeshop. "Are you there? Anne? Are you going to hang up on me?"

The crying stopped. "Hi, Miles, how are you?"

➧ It was Miles Kasendorf again. Miles Max Kasendorf. He had written his full name on a napkin when they had coffee in the English tearoom a thousand years ago, and a basket of rolls and biscuits. "What's your middle name, Anne? Or do you go by Annie? I've heard people call you Anne, but other people call you Annie." Annie Kane's middle name was Marie, but she had told Miles it was Fanny. At first, he didn't know what to say. Then he laughed so loud, the people in the restaurant had turned to look. "I like you," he said, "you're a riot."

➧ Miles asked where she was going after work, and if she hadn't made plans, would she meet him just for a drink in Cambridge—take a half hour—or, if she had more time, have dinner and maybe catch a film. One of the nurses had come down to get Barry out of the coffeeshop and back on the ward, but Barry didn't want to go. He was still carrying the cup and it took the aide, the nurse, and the receptionist, Mrs. McDonald, who rushed over from her desk, pushing from behind to get him out of the opening, across the corridor, and into the elevator. He was talking fast about his brother in Chepachet who was coming in the car to pick him up and take him to Mrs. Hogan's house: "Mrs. Hogan is my aunt on my father's side, cousin once removed, my aunt or my cousin; I'm *her* cousin," he explained to the receptionist, twisting his neck around to see her, "for Thanksgiving dinner." You bet your life, the receptionist said, and the elevator closed on her back until someone pressed the OPEN button and she jumped out. She was a middle-aged woman, very plain, with three kids in school and an ailing husband. A lot of the patients drifted downstairs because the coffeeshop was there, but also to chat with Mrs. McDonald, pass the time of day. She was one of the only people, Miss Kane noticed, who talked to them in a pleasant tone, no matter what they said in return.

She told Miles Kasendorf no. "Great. When do you get in?" Talking almost as fast as Barry, Miles said he got out of class and could get to Kenmore Square by 6, 6:15 at the latest and if this was convenient, he'd— "Or, would you rather I meet you in downtown Boston?" She said she didn't have time tonight. "Or Cambridge: it doesn't matter because I have a car; it's fine either way." He asked if 7 would be better. All right, she said. "If I'm late, go into Nini's; I'll look for you in Nini's."

Miss Kane went upstairs to the big ladies' room and sat down in a lounge chair. The nurses kept their things in here and snuck in during lunch to avoid the patients. The patients were very friendly at lunch and the nurses ended up sitting at one of the round tables jammed with ten or twelve patients, one on top of the other, jabbering all at once. But no one was in there so she felt free to do a little thinking. Miles M. Kasendorf was now twenty-five years old, still non-Catholic; hair, black and curly, skin very pink; when she first met him she had never seen anyone who looked like this before. Now everyone looked like him, except maybe Barry and Joey. He was from New York, the son of a psychiatrist and a heart specialist, the son of two doctors, and brother of Alfred Kasendorf, a doctor. His sister, Marcia A. Kasendorf, was a graduate student at Columbia University, and his baby brother, Mark Alan, was in prep school in Concord, Massachusetts. She crossed her legs on the lounge chair and threw an arm over her eyes. Now, his present girlfriend, Alexandra Browne Canfield, in the front of the house, was a medical student at Harvard; and his old girlfriend, Anne M. Kane, in the rear and out of school, was in mental health. She'd better watch out, she thought; she'd be talking out loud in a minute and laughing at nothing just like the patients.

She had come to their house, Anne Marie Kane, St. Edward's High, Radcliffe B.A., a wreck, made her room a goldenrod, skipped out of work to brood, was bad with money, untidy, secretive, ugly moods, lazy, and now going to steal away the boyfriend of Alex— and she had already *had* this boyfriend; it was just old Miles—right from under the girl's nose? And what would she get in return? Miss Kane had goosebumps on her arms as the door flung open on Mrs.

D'Ambra, who had just started back to work after a long siege with the lung, and behind her, Mary Mallon holding a brown bag full of something. Both were looking at Miss Kane, big as life, stretched out at her ease. And who was watching the art workshop all this time?

No one was in the art workshop. The patients had gone to Freeman's Park for a picnic and a birthday party. Miss Kane sat at one of the art tables and rested her head on her arms so she had a closeup view of the latest artwork by a new patient, a black kid, friend of Eddie's, who only drew heads from the back, circles covered with hair. It was like looking at wet wallpaper.

Thinking back, she was sorry she had been so mean to poor Miles, and was going to get him again. He didn't deserve it. Some people deserved it, but he didn't. It was no one's fault she was a fool, and certainly not poor Miles's fault, who was kind of a fool himself. Like most Harvard boys, he was fitted on a silver platter no bigger than the lid of a garbage can; he could fit on it if it was just himself and he wasn't too overweight and kept his feet tucked under; if he got too lively, he would tip and be drooling (a double espresso or Campari with ice?) down the front of him.

They had had the couple of dates, two or was it three? They were fools together and it was not such a bad memory, not all of it anyway. What is a memory? What are my memories that they would be like this, or am I getting them all wrong?

He had hung his pure black coat, soft on the outside, silky on the inside, on a peg in the back of the café. The bar, called The Parrot, was dark with a big copper coffee machine and small glass cups all around it, a menu on a chalkboard and a vase of flowers. This is a memory, I can feel it. Where am I? She waited for him with her hands folded on a little table. Next to them was a drink, red with ice, Cinzano, can you say that? Cinzano. That was it; here it was. Miles K. came to the table with a bottle of wine under his arm. "I haven't seen a bottle of this in a long time." He pulled it out to show her the label; it was a French label and the bottle was dusty. Mr. K. took a napkin and wiped the bottle. The waiter was standing behind him with a corkscrew and two glasses. He put them on the table. Miles was still wiping.

The waiter came back a minute later with a tall glass decanter. Miles talked to the waiter while he screwed the coil into the cork. The waiter put the full bottle against the candle and poured out a beautiful purple stream, watching the transfer through the flame. He took the old bottle away. Miles looked into the side of the decanter.

"He's going to rinse that other one out with a simple Bordeaux," he said with his finger raised, as if they had been talking for hours, but they hadn't talked at all. They had just arrived, straight from the library where he was playing records in the poetry room. She had seen him in there many times; he knew the man in charge of the poetry room and was always talking to him. One day he picked a chair near Miss Kane. He waited a minute, then pulled the book she was reading, *Art in East and West,* right out of her hands. "I know him," he said. "He's my neighbor. It's a landmark study, you know. After Rowland, nothing's been the same."

The waiter came back and poured the wine back into the old bottle. "Now we're just going to let it draw in some air," Mr. K. said, "and fill out. Take a sniff," he said, pushing the bottle toward Miss K.; "don't pick it up."

It smelled good. It had a muddy smell. Miles K. put the bottle down and reached across the table to wrap his big hand around the skinny hand already wrapped around something, a blue tissue, and ready to start shredding. Miles told her (when?) or had already told her or hadn't told her but was going to tell her that she was a different woman, not in the ordinary way, but in a way he recognized. She was different, slightly neurotic, and introverted; it was something he was used to in a female, he said, so not to be concerned about it: you don't want people to see into you, he said; you're all closed up, yet I can see you in there looking out. I see you inquiring into everything and seeing everything and that's what puts people off about you, but I like you. I'm looking too. He stopped. Then he started up again. But you're even more difficult than *I* am.

He was saying this, she figured, because she wasn't able to tell him what he wanted to know. He was asking do you like this, do you like that? East Coast or West Coast, camping or sailing, resorts in Maine or on the Keys, New York or San Francisco, Bose speakers or KLH, Porcellian or Fly, Lear or Othello, the Juilliard or the Guarneri, bourbon or rye, Billie Holliday or Sarah Vaughan, Buster Keaton or Harold Lloyd, *Potemkin* or *Children of Paradise,* bop or cool, Flaubert or Stendhal, Merleau-Ponty or Husserl, Poe in English or Poe in French, Astaire and Astaire or Astaire and Rogers, Cagney or Bogart, Glenlivet or Glenfiddich, Simon or Kael, aspirin or Bufferin, analysis or group, Disney or Warners, Amos or Andy, Berle or Kovacs, Pusey or Bok, Lawrence or Durrell, the O.T. or the N.T., Eisenhower or Truman, fresh water or salt water, Mailer or Heller, the Sox or the Yankees, French or Szechuan, Lochober's or Henri

Quatre, medieval or Renaissance, Furtwängler or Van Karajan, English saddle or western, Nikon or Hasselblad, Albers or Rothko, Shakespeare or the Bible, methadone or benign neglect, Friedan or Greer, Collins or Mitchell, Clapton or Hendrix, SDS or PL, fountain or ballpoint, Willie McTell or Tampa Red, Ravi Shankar or Ali Akbar Khan, Redbone or Cooder, Firesign Theater or Mr. Natural?

She listened. Sometimes she made a choice, sometimes she said she didn't like either. Remembering these, she wished she had said: Miles, which do you like better? sticks or stones, chicken or turkey, Limbo or Purgatory, Cap'n Kangaroo or Miss Frances, Pawtucket or Central Falls, Girl Scouts or Girl Guides, orange slices or rootbeer barrels, brown eggs or white eggs, Scarborough or East Matunuck, Friday or Saturday, Bishop Sheen or Cardinal Cushing, *Glamour* or *Mademoiselle,* cancer or heart disease, Jello or Junket, fruit cocktail or individual pies, Tums or Rolaids, water from the faucet or water with ice, jacks or jumprope, Mogen David or Manischewitz, Wonder or Sunbeam, Haystack Calhoun or the Masked Marvel, "Beat the Clock" or "Concentration," grade 4 or grade 5, SAT or PSAT, Candyland or Chutes and Ladders, beans and hotdogs or beans and franks?, but she didn't. She listened to him. What was he saying? He was saying how different she was and how hard it was to tell what she was thinking.

No he wasn't. He had changed the subject. I don't always go out like this, he was saying; I don't go out at all; I stay home most of the time and read James and Dostoevsky; those are my favorites. I bet they're your favorites, too; you're just the type.

He was staring at her and saying how oftentimes he would prefer staying home in bed with a late James than going out (he had already said this and here he was saying it again) to be bored. She was wondering if she should feel insulted. He stopped talking. "Let me ask you something," he said. "Don't be offended. I can see you're going to be offended, but don't be. I can't help but ask you this." He stopped again. "Are you a little in love with me?"

Miss Kane couldn't answer this question. She had on the tip of her tongue something else: *The Bostonians, Washington Square, The Idiot, Notes from the Underground, Daisy Miller, The Brothers K, Portrait of a Lady,* but never finished *The Ambassadors.*

Questions about subjects were starting to come up and she didn't always have an answer to give. Sometimes she didn't know exactly what it was they were talking about: movies, music, books, people, things, drinks, food, dressmakers, potters, printmakers, intellectuals, and she was starting to lie or hide the fact that she hadn't heard of whatever it was; but Henry James and Dostoevsky she had heard of and had read a lot of their books, although she hadn't talked about them that often.

It was funny that now these subjects *never* came up. No one asked about anything. No, she had had the one conversation with Mary Mallon, who hated a thick book and especially James, and was a little suspicious, Miss Kane could tell, of the kind of person who would carry a book day in and day out, *The Awkward Age*—"Are you really reading that?"

But Miles liked to read. He admitted it. She could picture him in his room; big piles of library books all over the floor and windowsills, old and musty, some open, some with bookmarks, and him stretched out on his thin bed under an old army blanket, tee shirt, black socks sticking out. It was a funny picture and she realized it was a picture in *Life* magazine of a sailor resting. "Why are you smiling?" he had said, and there was the waiter asking Miles if he could pour the wine for them.

"You haven't answered my question," he said, taking the bottle out of the waiter's hand, pouring a little bit into his own glass, swishing it around and taking a sip. He motioned to the waiter and now they both had half-filled glasses of dark-red wine. Mr. Kasendorf picked up his glass and clinked it, "To you," against Miss Kane's. "You're blushing a little," he said.

He took another sip and looked away. He knew some of the people here, he said, sitting at the other tables all squashed together. He nodded at them to prove it.

"You haven't answered my question," he said. He looked right at her face. She drank a little more wine and looked at him through the bottom of the glass. Something—a hand—was on her leg. "Maybe you should start, if you're embarrassed, by asking me if I'm in love with you." "Are you?" she said. He smiled and drank the rest of his wine.

Miss Kane got up to go to the ladies' room. Miles K. held her back; people were looking. "You're not going to get out of this so easily," he said; "I'll just ask you again when you come out." "Okay," she said.

Miss Kane came back to the table—it was nice to be liked—and drank the wine, looked out the window while Miles was thinking. People were walking past the cafe, men in puffy parkas, women in black with long black or long blonde hair. Was she in love with him?

She slid her eyes over to look at his face. It was a nice face, not hand-some, but . . . A girl walking in wearing a pirate hat with a big feather was heading toward their table—someone Miss Kane knew—but then veered away and went to another table.

They had changed the record; it was classical at first, but now it was jazz and Miles was talking about the acts he had caught in the 60s in high school ("In high school?"): Brubeck and Monk, Mingus and Parker, Gillespie and Shorter, alive and in their prime. He had walked in on a jam session once with Lester Young in broad daylight, midtown Manhattan—*that* was something. She wondered if he might be named after Miles Davis. "Life," he was saying, cut-ting this question off, "has been more than boring since then, now that they're all dead or nearly dead, and New York an impossible place to live with even half a million; no middle class there anymore, know what I mean?"

"Do I *ever*," they heard. "I lived there last summer, stayed in my father's place, but I couldn't stand it, so I got my own"—it was the pirate hat, Nell Beechcroft, that's who it was—"just for the summer, a few months, and by the end—oh," she said, extending a slim hand to Miles Davis—no, Kasendorf—"Nell Beechcroft; we haven't met but I think I've seen you before; anyway, as I was saying, by the end of the summer, a hideous summer, I was eating nothing but cereal, sometimes not even with milk, and ice cream cones, a pizza if I was lucky."

It *was* Nell Beechcroft, someone Annie had met her first day, an-other transfer student, Smith College, beautiful and thin with straight blonde hair and all in black with ballet slippers; she gave Annie a kiss, then knelt by the table so her chin came up to the edge and looked at Miles. "You don't have a cigarette, do you?"

"Don't move," he said, putting a hand on the long hair, getting up and walking off.

"Annie," Nell said in a whisper, "I haven't seen you in so long. What are you doing?"

Miss Kane was starting to say—. "Let's meet for coffee and we'll talk. I've moved off campus; did you know? Let me give you my number." Annie Kane handed the kneeling girl a piece of lined paper from a notepad and Nell wrote her name, two addresses and phone numbers in an unreadable but pretty handwriting, just as a package of Gauloises fell onto the table. Miles sat down. Nell Beechcroft was flipping a long strand of hair over her shoulder and shaking her shoulders so the hair would fall in a smooth panel. Miles opened the pack and lit a cigarette for Nell and one for himself, both in his mouth at the same time. "Will you join us?" he said, pulling a nearby chair until it almost tipped over.

"I can't really," Nell Beechcroft said. "I just wanted to say hello," blowing a stream of smoke toward Miles's face. "You never see this girl," still looking at Miles, "she's in hiding, I think, or would like to be." Nell jumped up and rustled away.

They both watched until Nell Beechcroft was settled at her table, and never looked their way again.

"She's a beautiful girl, do you know her?" Miles said, moving the hand over again to its place under the table. Miss Kane took another sip of wine. Mr. K. leaned farther over. Miss Kane, although she was embarrassed to look right at his face, saw that his eyes were red. "Anne Marie."

What?

"Has anyone ever made love to you?"

The blue tissue she was holding was a round marble of tightness. It rolled onto the table. It was wet, too. She couldn't think of anything to say.

"I want you to trust me," Miles K. said; "I don't know if you do."

I trust you, Miss Kane said.

"You're young. I can see that. You're nodding yes, but you're even younger than you think you are. Don't feel bad. I don't mind."

He paused, then took the hand from below the table and put it with the other one, on top of her hand. The blue ball was still adrift. "Tell me the truth now. Have you ever—?"

Miss Kane was trusting him. She was trusting him and liking him for saying such kind things. "No," she said. Yes would have been true too.

❦ This was a certain kind of thinking, and plenty of time to do it in the silent car next to Miss Mallon, who was driving carefully and breathing heavily through her nose. And if you think this way, it's not a bad story. Thinking this way there was no need to meet Miles Kasendorf in the magazines at Nini's, or for a drink at The Parrot, and for a film and a dinner, then or ever again. She had done enough.

THE WORKHOUSE

I saw her scraping the floor with her nails, that's how good she cleans. I told her if you clean that deep into the grooves of nature, the dirt will be that much eagerer to climb back in. Oh, another of your theories, she said, and not as rigorous as I have grown accustomed. Well, do it then, I said.

She stood up from the hands and knees, knees having the pattern of nailed in dirt and nothing of cleanliness, but where does it come from, Helen, all this dirt?

We sat at the tabletop, her face clammy but eyes heated with love of knowledge. I opened a palm and laid a finger across it. First—but there was someone, Eddie, at the door.

Sit down, Eddie, I said to the kid with the endless life of combat in the dirt, nails bitten to the bed and under the bed. Tell your mother here how they put their little blackened hands under the window no matter how tight you've nailed them shut and inch across a beaten track of dust and hairs gone unnoticed in the baseboard groove.

I don't know, Helen, he said; who's got the mind for it? His mother was on her knees again using that rough tongue of hers on the slats. Well, sit and listen, I said to him, learn something new today.

A long time ago—but that was the door and Feeble the cat padded grime into the fine-licked floor.

Ginny, I said, take your tongue and whisk that path the cat made before someone—him, pointing to Eddie, running his little finger, a bloody stub, along the aluminum fender of the tabletop and sucking that filth out—tracks it in.

I began once more while she had the popsicle stick dipped in blueing and was scraping the soles of Eddie's shoes and listening to hear if she had gotten it all.

Kids, I said, love dirt like they were made of it. This is where the problem begins. She had a hand vacuum with a special ear brush attachment and was deep inside the boy scanning for and parting away organ for organ, looking for what would be termed slime or chalky resin.

Carriers, they are, I said, lifting my big crepe shoes onto the table so they could identify in a superficial way the kinds and quality of sediment and ordure I picked up in my life and the way I lived, which I told them wasn't fit for an animal, a whole lifetime of unwanted inorganic matter—mineral life, Eddie said; shut your fresh mouth, I said—caking a layer of unhappiness on my walls, but here, with Ginny, this was heaven, the way heaven should have been before the rags, lumps and sand and their own specially fertile life came via paradise, that garden of shit.

Don't encourage her, I told young Eddie, who had taken a pin to the rubber tread on the refrigerator door and was doing a taste test. An ointment for this, he said, and they were both involved with sweating blood and tears, as they used to say, to find and apply the only way to clean the deep grids of horror in the refrigerator tread: a haemoglobin-saline solvent applied with teeth and lips, with the tongue to hold the findings.

Sit, sit, I said, sit before I lose my mind with the infinity of small tasks you're finding to make life worth living, that's my theory, Ginny, like it or not. They sat, Ginny with her head down on the table for a closer look at the underground. Eddie, the jerk, I could kill that kid, was sorting through his mother's hair which had gone virtually unattended since I had arrived that morning with my coffee cup.

So Helen, she finally said, her eyes open, her face—Eddie's face, too—flushed and magnetizing every particle of gunk or mote available within that slight electromagnetic field. I watched them land like insects on an insect electrocution rod. Too bad, Ginny, I said, you're making work for yourself just being alive and pumping that foul generator and sewage system attached. Just sit, vegetate or rust for a minute and give me a chance to lay out the theory you desire.

But they, Ginny and Eddie—Feeble was licking particulates from his flank—couldn't sit. Work is life, I said; I'd never deny it, just as God, or Gut as you say, sent the flies to make this sanitary life what it is. In the crack of the table leaf they found their joy in the dirt jelly that abided there and they tested a variety of implements, catching the precipitate in an old hairnet, tying it up with a nylon of Ginny's, and out to that hive, that hothouse the family called—but they didn't really call it anything. The men in body outfits with face parts came to port it away and the family could start over accumulating, rubbing, scraping, siphoning, sucking and so on. It was a cyclic affair, this kind of clean life they had, and it was a life unlike the infested but null pattern of my own, which is why I came as often as I did, offering my private history and archives of collaboration with the kind of dirt, filth, grease, crud, dust, mud, shit, rot, warp, internal and external corruption and addition—foreign bodies of various kinds. Talk is cheap, I told them, it isn't life, not the kind of life you have.

But they didn't have time for me unless I was addressing their topic, and my ideas were not always worthy of them.

Like once I had suggested they wrap, lay, cover, drape, line, and otherwise pervert every household surface: smooth, corrugated, horizontal, vertical, plane, spherical appliance or structural unit with a form of paper or fabric, thus forming a false surface for the daily bombardment by things, fluids, fluctuants, solids, particulates, mixtures, gases, evacuations of certain kinds that invited removal. Then, remove, Ginny—Eddie, you too—and the beginning of a new dirt.

For a minute, I swear their attention was mine. Their eyes flicked and a shifty energy galvanized the latent pourriture everywhere in life, also the invasion of larger matter, which was distracting enough to make her, if not him, lose faith in ideas and resolves—him more than her because younger and newer to resolves—to turn face, inward and outward to the thing they loved most.

So I slip away, quiet in my deep rifts and veins and darkened reality, but not untouched, not uncorroded by the harsh but cleansing alkaline rinse of that house, its atmosphere.

ROVE her to college. Packed the car and sat in front with an extra little suitcase on the floor, the makeup case, hard blue, with the mirror, and all the things tossed in there in a big jumble. It didn't matter; they'd all have to be taken out and arranged (her mother was stopping for gas at Tony's Texaco: Hi, Al. Mrs. Kane, how do; what can I do for you? Hi there, Anne Marie, got your suitcase I see. She's going to college. Oh? Up Massachusetts way, full scholarship. How about that.) and the thought of a new place: bureau, closet, drawer, bathroom, for the old things: hairbrush, powder, soap on a rope, made her want to get out here at Tony's, walk home. She curled the toes of both feet, then rolled up the window so she could watch Al, Tony's helper, but not have to talk to him. They didn't have to go away; they could stay here. Out this window she could see a corner of the First National, the bakery shop and just the sign for the cobbler's. On her mother's side, past her mother's head, was another cobbler's and a children's store, the newspaper and cigar store, big as a hallway and always smelled good, and the drugstore. If I get out and lie under the car— but Al had given her mother the change and they were pulling out, just the two of them, in the green and white Ford beachwagon, the best used car they had ever gotten: they said this, her mother or father—especially him—every time they got into it. A cloth scapular was hanging from the rear-view mirror and a marble was in the groove on the dashboard, the ashtray filled with cigarette butts, although they were both cutting down to a pack a day, less. Inside the glove compartment was a jumble of papers and junk: nothing worked, not even the flashlight. Her mother was lighting a True Blue with her car lighter and that awful tired smell was coming into the car; Anne Marie closed her eyes but stifled the sigh that had started and was going to be big and hopeless. "You're not tired already, are you?" I have a headache. "You always have a headache when you have to do anything new. Why don't you just look forward to it and be happy you're going. No one else is getting to go. We're all staying here, same old thing. You're the lucky one." I know. "Why don't you enjoy it for a change." I *am* enjoying it. "No, you're not; I can see you're not. You're just like your father, can't enjoy anything, even when it's handed to you on a silver platter."

This was true, like everything her mother said was true. It was coming to her: she could picture it, on a big tray all carved and heavy, part of a silver service her mother would love to have; all the aunts had one; you couldn't be Irish without one; you couldn't be Irish if you didn't have a silver service, silver flatware, a Belleek cup and saucer with tiny shamrocks and a Christmas crèche of Hummel figures, or any figures; if you had Hummel figures, it was so much better and you got that much more credit. They didn't have any of these things, and it wasn't that they didn't want them: they all did, her mother, father, her big brother Jimmy and little sister Ellen. They owned their own house, yes, but didn't have the things to go in it. She was getting away now and didn't have to live with it anymore, although her mother reminded her every day that family is all you really have; you can count on family the way you can't count on anyone else, so Anne Marie knew things were going to get worse. Even so, on this silver platter, heavy and rich, was coming a college education at a ritzy—as her brother put it—girls' school up in Boston. Jimmy wasn't going; he had barely made it into the local j.c., and right out on his ear a month later, all F's, and Ellen was still too little, hated school, but was glad Anne Marie, fat and homely, was getting out so she could have the small flowered-print room all to herself and spread her dolls out and her private things, without interference from a big teenager, messy and ugly-tempered. The two sisters, Anne Marie and Ellen Jane, hated each other and had many fights and screaming matches; neither of them liked the brother either, so sallow and mean he was, dirty mouth, a squealer, and with a terrible temper. He and the grandmother were allies and did everything together; Ellen got along with the mother because they were both quiet and sarcastic. But Anne Marie and her father had no friends in the family, no one to take their part. They were the problems, they caused the trouble, they were the ones you had to cater to, the moody ones who spoiled everything for everyone else. But at least, Miss K. was thinking, one of them was getting out and on a silver platter like a flying carpet.

They were cruising and the front end of the car began to shimmy, so they had to slow down and let the other cars—some of them were filled with dresses and suitcases and had the names of colleges scotch-taped to the back window—pass. They were reading these names and getting giddy: Wellesley—look at that one, imagine the sweaters she has; see, a Row D'Ilin license: Barrington! MIT, what's that? Massachusetts something, a teachers' college, Harvard, Newton, Christ College—Look, that's you; look, just like you in there. It was a white Cadillac with license plate: Songs. Do you think that's their name? Look, the whole backseat's full of dresses. You better not stand next to her at the dances; see if you can see what she has on. They couldn't keep up with the white Cadillac but Anne Marie thought she saw a pink angora sweater and a little matching pillbox. Get out of here, her mother said; you can't see that, and they both started laughing: don't make me laugh, I can't drive straight. And a tiny pink poodle on the skirt. Stop. Pink patent-leather party slippers with pink silk stockings. Try to act your age; she might be your roommate, then what are you going to do? but added, pink matching underpants and slip and pink pearl strand—This is making me sick. Don't worry; that's not half as bad as it's going to be, Anne Marie, you're going in with doctors' daughters, lawyers', politicians'. Who do you think can afford to send their kid, three thousand bucks a year, to an out-of-state college like this, room and board, pocket money? You're out of your league; your parents couldn't afford to send you to a place like this in a million years. But, you've got the brain; you got the scholarships, don't forget that. Anne M. Kane knew her mother was feeling a lot of relief that *she* didn't get the scholarships. Someone got them, someone would go. Someone would go and come back and tell her about it.

Are we there yet? Look at the map. Anne Marie had the map, Massachusetts—Rhode Island—Connecticut right on her lap and they had drawn a pencil line from Providence to Kingsford: Route 1, Route 75, Route 128, Route 12, Route 19A, College Drive and there it was: you couldn't see it on the map, but Anne Marie remembered that it was on a big lawn with a round tower and an old-fashioned mansion. A pretty girl, junior year, had shown her and her mother around the day last spring they came all the way out for a visit and an interview. "What'd she say her name was?" her mother must have asked a million times on the way back and afterwards. They were still trying to think of it a week before she was set to go for good: Goreeta something? Gretta. No, it wasn't Gretta; I would have remembered that; that's easy. Doretta? No! They had laughed themselves silly one day when her mother came upstairs where Anne Marie was sewing a label on her coat with her name printed on it: you were supposed to sew a label into everything, but it seemed so tedious that she stapled some of them: won't that scratch you? her mother said. Anne Marie said she didn't care, but then she pried some of them out, ripped her new underwear and was disgusted by the whole thing and decided it wasn't worth it, but then felt like sewing in just one. Her mother was out of breath because she tore up the stairs with the dustrag in her hand and a can of Pledge: "Anne

Marie." "What?" "I know what her name is." "What name?" "You know. That pretty girl who showed us all over the college." "What's her name?" "Garcia. Wasn't that it?" Anne Marie's head fell onto the coat, just missing the needle. Her shoulders were shaking. "Look up," her mother said. Anne Marie, big red face laughing and choking, saw her mother with the pincurl scarf, her old eyeglasses with the black frames all slanted to a point and that look she had on her face; she burst out laughing so hard she though she might throw up, and still laughing. "You can't call her that." "Well, what's her name? You tell me."

Anne Marie was thinking about exactly this question when they missed the exit for Route 12, which scared her mother: what if they got lost way out here? Who would find them? and they were so relieved when the mother veered into another exit and found, Hail Mary full of grace the Lord is with thee, another exit that flipped them around until they were going back on Route 128 and, Anne Marie kept explaining over and over, were sure to run into the exit they had missed. No one said a word.

There it was; they both screamed, the mother took the exit, and safe. So happy, they stopped at the very next restaurant, out in the middle of nowhere, Christ College orientation for freshmen begun and already way ahead and Anne Marie way behind, to eat a nice lunch. I thought of her name. "What name?" That girl—you know, Garcia. "Oh her. I don't even care anymore." Do you want to hear her name? "Not particularly." Are you sure? "Just tell me." Dorita Garcia. At first, the mother laughed and Anne Marie laughed; then, Mrs. Kane looked at her daughter, stupid and silly on her way to college: "Smarten up; you don't want them to see you like that. A lot of them could be in this restaurant right now, you don't know."

No one was in the restaurant. It was a pancake restaurant and Anne Marie ordered blueberry pancakes; she ate too many, no one could stop her, then felt full of pain and headaches the rest of the day. They were quiet over lunch; they just ate and left. They were quiet the rest of the way to Kingsford. It wasn't far; after Route 12, you could just follow the cars; each car had a college girl and a mother and father; sometimes the college girl was sitting in between them— sometimes she was in the front with her mother in the back. They followed these cars: Buicks, Chryslers, Cadillacs, Chevrolets, no beachwagons except the one, up the winding drive; all over the campus were college girls and their parents lugging suitcases and looking strained. Anne Marie had never seen so many pretty girls in such beautiful clothes: all the colors she had seen in the magazines—plum, wheat, forest green, cherry, cranberry—were here, and some of the exact outfits she had seen. They followed the string of cars to a big parking lot and someone started tooting at them for gawking instead of finding a parking space and getting out of the way. They found a space and sat in the car. "You get out and see where we are." No. "Go ahead." I don't want to. "You can't stay in here all day." Anne Marie Kane, eighteen, with a cold clammy hand and a huge indigestion pulled the handle of the car door only to discover her new flower-printed maroon shirtwaist had a big green mark from being caught in the greasy door. There was no need to touch it with a cloth or a tissue: it was there forever. "Are you all right?" Anne Marie looked up and was sorry to be looking into a nun's face with her eyes full of tears. It was a small, lively nun: Sister Domitilla (Tortilla, Anne Marie made a mental note to transmit this name to her mother) who shook Anne Marie's arm: "Come on, you'll be okay; this is just the beginning." The nun hadn't noticed the grease spot so Anne Marie thought maybe it was invisible if you didn't know it was there. The nun gave her a hug with one arm, then peeked in the car windows. Anne Marie could see her mother looking the other way, trying to pretend she didn't see any of this: she was uncomfortable with nuns, and had explained to her daughter that she wasn't a religious fanatic like some people she knew. She hadn't gone to "sister school," as they used to call it and as far as she was concerned, hadn't missed anything. Sister Domitilla stood up, gave Anne Marie some quick instructions about where her residence hall was and hurried away. She told Anne Marie she was an instructor in physics and was looking forward to seeing this young lady, a math major, in the freshman physics class come Monday morning.

Anne Marie stood on the sidewalk a minute. Her mother was motioning her, but she took a minute to look around at the people swarming into a new building, three stories and very long, with one big window where you could see stairs and a hallway with people swarming around in there leaning over long wooden tables. There was a long line that went down the stairs and out the side door. Anne Marie, opening the car door, told her mother it was bedlam. "Well, that's too bad; you have to stay anyway." They carried the suitcases and cardboard boxes across the parking lot and into an old brick building, climbed the three flights of stairs and dragged the big suitcase down a long dark corridor with green linoleum and dim overhead lights to room 302. "What does it say on your letter?" 302.

"Well, this is 302," Mrs. Kane said and started opening the door, but Anne Marie pulled it closed. No! "What do you mean no?" What if somebody is there already? "So what. It's your room isn't it?" she said in a loud voice anyone could hear.

The door opened and there was who Anne Marie thought it was: Margaret C. H. Kelly, the roommate. She was from Rhode Island and Anne Kane had met her one afternoon, as the college suggested they do, in downtown Providence. First, Margaret C. H. (as they called her in the Kane house) told Anne M. Kane that people who knew her, her friends at Elmhurst Academy (Anne Marie's mother screamed when she heard that. A boarding school! Your little room-mate went to a boarding school.), called her March; that settled, March took Anne Marie Cathleen Kane to where her father worked: Bache, the doorway said; Anne Marie couldn't even pronounce it and hoped March would say it first. Her father, Mr. Everett Clarence Kelly, worked on the New York Stock Exchange, but he had a down-town office. "This must be Anne Marie," Mr. March—no, Kelly—said, shaking her hand. He was a tall man with two pairs of glasses; one was pushed up on his head, the other, small glasses, only half a lens in each, were on his nose.

Her mother wanted to know every detail about the stockbroker ("What is a stockbroker, do you know?" Anne Marie said she did but, as usual, couldn't explain it very well, so what good was all this knowledge?), and the stockbroker's daughter—what was her name again? To keep her mother from hearing her name and adapting it to suit her funnybone, Anne Marie Kane always referred to her room-mate as Margaret Kelly, a name March would have hated, but since she hated Anne Marie Kane, A student and sycophant, anyway, be-fore too long, it didn't make any difference what she called her. Her mother, after a while, referred to the roommate as The Kelly Girl.

Looking back, Miss Kane wasn't sure what had gone wrong. She wasn't sure whether March had decided in advance to despise her, or had been prompted by one of Miss Kane's obnoxious and sickening words, looks, or actions, which she was in a position to see and to see every day at close range: her bed was four feet away, although she, March, spent very little time in the room, either a) because Anne Marie Kane was there being conscientious or b) because Miss Kane's mother had picked out the bedspreads and curtains and they were hideous. (March Kelly never put hers on the bed, but rolled it up and stuffed it in the closet, which made Anne Marie Kane , 18½, eight weeks into college and already 10 pounds overweight after slimming down so well over the summer, feel sad for her mother—who didn't even know, way back in Providence, she was being belittled—every time she laid eyes on the foamy mound.) It took Kane, as some of the hallmates called her—the ones who liked her a little because she was smart, and popular at the mixers when none of the rest of them were. She had explained that it was easy to fix yourself up for one night: makeup, a dress with a slimming cut but a bright, noticeable color, and it didn't matter what you really looked like; all the boy saw was this—a week and a half to see how hideous the bedspread was, looked from a certain (March, Eleanor, Phoebe, Isabel, Jo, Carole and Jane; 302, 306, 305, 301) angle, and equally hideous some other things she had brought with her, but she couldn't bring herself to strip it—big cabbage flowers on cheap material with a flimsy, all-synthetic lining—from the bed, although she never made the bed so you couldn't really see it all rolled in a bundle under the sheet and blanket with a week's worth of clothing rolled in there with it.

It started right away that night; all the mothers and fathers had gone home and the dorm was a little quiet for a half hour: Miss Kane didn't feel that sad; it was fun to see all these new clothes come out of the box and suitcase and find places to put them, but March Kelly, she could see, was crying in a silent way. It would be the nice thing to say something, but Miss Kane couldn't think of what to say so kept unpacking. The Kelly girl left the room after a few minutes without even saying goodbye. Miss Kane could hear her next door chatting with the two roommates there, a girl from Massachusetts and a girl from Connecticut. The girl from Connecticut, fat with long brown hair and a sweet face, had a voice you could hear anywhere and Miss Kane could hear it saying: You can come in with us, Barbara and me, anytime you want, so don't worry. Miss Kane was surprised by this, and by its sharp tone. She had been trying to hang all the skirts on a big skirt hanger with thousands of separate clips; it was almost filled and the last skirt, green, draped on the floor. No time for tears now, her mother had said, climbing into the car, and Miss Kane didn't feel the need, although she could see her mother's eyes were red, but now—ten minutes before dinner—was not the time either, so it had to be put off. Plus, that was the door and March Kelly's sulky face asking her if she were going over to the union. Yes. Well, you can come with us if you want to. Miss Kane put the full skirt hanger down and followed the three girls, who were joined by four more girls from the other end and a few others until all the girls from their end were together in a big pack, and Miss Kane, to her surprise, in there with them, for the first time in her life, part of a clique or gang. Later, she found out there were others like her, including an ugly girl whose clothes were all thin and hung off her in loose drapes and folds, a little grimy looking; Hilda and Trudy, one tomboy with scraggly blonde hair and a pug nose and her roommate, a thick slack-haired girl, devoted to the Sacred Heart, her side of the room filled with pictures and altars, and just here for a year before entering the convent in Peabody; and some others, included just for the numbers, to fill out the pack marching to dinner and breakfast with loud voices and laughs, noticeable by everyone and leading to—what surprised Miss Kane more than anything because she knew how angry and sullen, and how unfriendly and sad the girl was—the election of March Kelly to student body president and head of the national student congress. *That* was why, she told her mother a year later, when she could get her mother to listen to her, which wasn't that often—she had other things to do than listen to the complaints of a girl lucky enough to go to college in the first place: you made your bed, now lie in it—Anne Kane was included in anything these girls did. If it was anything public, March was friendly to her so people would see she was popular with *everybody*; if it was just a little something going on at the end of their corridor, she wasn't. In fact, none of these girls talked to Anne Kane except in a brusque or awkward way when, for some reason, she was thrown in with one of them, and they had to talk. It was not as much fun as people thought, being in college. It was misery, and some mornings Miss Kane was so sad, her contact lenses got all steamed over and she couldn't see the instructor or take good notes until after lunch when they got unsteamed; and tired, staying up late every night to learn every single fact they told her: she loved all her teachers and was afraid of them, and no matter how hard she worked, she knew they were still ahead.

The teachers at Christ were all young, or mostly young, and not all of them were nuns. One of them was Dr. Teesin, straight from Harvard, intellectual history, history of the western world, starting at the beginning. What? her mother had said; with Adam and Eve? Before then, Miss Kane said, way before then. What's before then? The Stone Age, the Iron Age, Miss Kane said, although she wasn't sure they were before or after Adam and Eve. Even though this was a Catholic college, Christ College was, Adam and Eve weren't considered the beginning of anything. Nobody was that certain anymore of a beginning: people had their ideas, but all their ideas didn't come together very smoothly in a nice story you could accept, or she could get her mother to accept. Dr. Teesin, tall and in a suit, with a dry, sarcastic voice Miss Kane began to like after a while, went fast over the beginning until he got up to the part he liked, the Middle Ages, with interesting theories of what people were like, very organized theories, Miss Kane thought, as were the theories about the Renaissance, and very easy to keep track of. She had never been good at dates; it was easier to remember theories and stick them in a big time period: Italian Renaissance, nineteenth-century Europe. Dr. Teesin talked for an hour and they were supposed to take notes of what he said and memorize it all, everything he said three hours a week and 15 weeks a semester. Miss Kane had never loaded her head with so many facts, and more of them were always coming. At first she looked over these notes in the evenings, sitting in the empty library, and then reading the big heavy textbook, which repeated what the notes said. This was an easy way to remember. But after a while, there were other things to do in the evenings, other studying and other things in general, so these notes just piled up and her handwriting was getting faster and worse, so it was harder to make them out. She still read his books—they were interesting books, not boring at all—but a lot of other things were getting mixed in with history, not just things in these books, but outside of them too.

At first, she had no friends, no one to pal around with; she just studied her books, ate dinner and lunch and got fatter, drank coffee in the student union and spent the night at a big table in the library watching the juniors and seniors, so neat they were and pretty with pins on their sweaters and diamond rings, able to sit with a book for hours; not all restless and itchy like Miss Kane, who had to get up and walk around every ten minutes and there was nothing to look at in this library, plus the nuns discouraged aimless roaming. One night, she saw March Kelly in there; she wasn't inside, she was outside, looking in the window, and looking at what? March Kelly never studied and started bragged about this from the first day—she hated teachers, even these different ones, not all nuns, and not mean; and she hated school, but she loved life in the dorm, Miss Kane could see this, and she loved what they called extracurricular activities: clubs, sports, after-lunch and after-supper meetings, and excursions. It was her aim, she had told Miss Kane when she was still talking to her, and she did once in a while when they would get in bed, turn out the lights and March would be homesick and unable to sleep, to get elected to the Social Committee. Miss Kane wouldn't even have heard of the Social Committee if it hadn't been for Mary

Jane Mahoney, her big sister, a tall junior with blonde hair, who worked in the cafeteria for spending money, and spent the money on clothes. Mary Jane knew everybody and was a lot of fun, Miss Kane could see that from the beginning: she loved dates and loved the boys from Holy Cross and Boston College and had a boyfriend in each one. *This*, she told her little sister whom she was very nice to, and didn't seem to realize no one else was so why bother, was what you paid attention to. Miss Kane, who was anxious to meet boys and had been all her life, knew this was true. One of the ways to do it, and meet the right kind of boy: tall, Irish, penny loafers, a car and a sport, a little on the fast side, but with a good front, a little money— Miss Kane knew the categories and the overall effect and liked it— was to be on the Social Committee and invite them to dances and mixers, to be in the position of organizer, Mary Jane explained, and her roommate, Susan—just as cute only brunette; they both wore the same clothes: A-line wool skirts and matching sweaters with round-collared blouses, sometimes with a monogram, sometimes not, a flat gold circle pin, also with a monogram all stenciled with curly letters, knee socks, and Weejun loafers, sometimes with a penny slot, sometimes with a tassle—chimed in. *This* is what, Miss Kane thought, a roommate should be, but first you had to be the kind of person, a live wire, a gallivanter, to attract and keep a roommate like this; you had, at the very least, to have the right clothes; you had to play bridge during the day instead of studying, get a tan in April with a big aluminum-foil shield, you had to keep getting pinned and by different boys, have a thousand pairs of skimpy Pappagallo flats, many cable-knit sweaters and a place to keep them all fluffed and folded, nice smooth skin, natural-colored hair in a perfect blonde pageboy, skinny legs to dance to all the latest soul music, the nerve to sign out for an overnight, to go all the way, stopping just before the end, then rush back to campus in a pure linen suit and parade into chapel five minues before the eleven o'clock Mass not a hair out of place. Miss Kane knew these things, and she knew Mary Jane and Susan were good at all of it, so when they told her how easy it was to get elected to Sosh, and when you did, then just call up the boys at Holy Cross, smart enough and cool enough to be elected to their own Sosh, and arrange things with them, and before you knew it, they'd ask you out on a date and you wouldn't even have to get on the bus and drive to Worcester to meet a real drag; the Sosh guy would come and take you to Boston in his Mustang; she understood this, but even with Mary Jane and Susan pulling, a type like herself would never in a million years get elected to Sosh, even though it would be nice, she knew it would.

In the meantime, she went on the bus to these mixers, and liked going. They advertised them on the bulletin board next to the mail-boxes where everyone went every day in a big mass, stampeding down the metal steps. She'd look for sign of a mixer, then check the mailbox. There was hardly ever a letter. Her mother wrote a short note once a week with a folded-up five dollar bill in a piece of news-paper, and her aunt and uncle would sent a card when it was close to a holiday, but the mailbox was mostly empty. She always opened it and stuck her arm in. It was worth taking the time, after checking the mailbox, to read the items on the bulletin board again because some of the crowd fresh out of the eleven o'clock class, and with one hour before the one o'clock class—and everybody had classes all day long, if you went to them and everyone did because there was no place to hide: the dorm nun checked every room and someone else was stationed in the coffee shop and student union—had pounded up these stairs and out and you had a moment's peace. Miss Kane would stand and read all the boring things, CCD, year abroad, Peace Corps, *Time* and *Newsweek*, Chaplain's letter, alumnae news, and wait while the screaming packs of girls streamed down the path to the union, a square brick building the nuns were always bragging about because it was new and expensive and they had it built with money from a fund-raising campaign they had designed and run themselves, the Little Sisters of St. Joseph, which contained a big deep empty room like a gym with windows up at the ceiling and a checkerboard of tables and chairs tightly packed together for the thousand boarders. It was very plain and very noisy: half of the lunch hour was spent standing in a thick line with an empty tray. Miss Kane hated lunch, dinner, and breakfast because she had no one to eat with and no one to stand with. In a place where everyone had friends—there were enough friends to go around of every kind and plenty of time to make them—she had no friends. By the time she realized the girls at her end of the corridor were never going to change their minds and be friendly, no matter what, it was too late to look elsewhere: everyone had already found friends and a group to fit into. She didn't mind this: there were other things to do, and hardly enough time to do them, but she didn't like to make a specta-cle of how alone she was three times a day seven days a week, when even the brains found the other brains, the jerks found the jerks, and Trudy and Hilda walked everywhere side by side.

She hadn't really expected to make any friends; in high school, she had only had the one friend and that friend was hurt she had gone to an out-of-state college when no one else did; not that that friend, Mary L. Conley, was all that surprised when she did it. Anne Kane was getting too big for Providence and everyone could see that. Whenever the nuns wanted to send one of them out into the world, science fair, debating team, Alliance Française, just to show that Catholics could speak French too and had a lab with their physics and chemistry, four years of Latin and penmanship, they sent out Anne Kane in full uniform. The girl had gotten a taste, Mary L. Conley could see this, for the la-de-dah; no matter how many stories Mary told her about how flat on their faces the mighty fall, especially coming from *this* neighborhood, Anne Kane had to see for herself, so Mary L. Conley, who had taken care of her up to now—so flighty and so restless—let her go, knowing she'd never be happy leaving the neighborhood.

Mary had told her this in her harsh but funny terms that last Communion breakfast, and the last time they, she and Mary, would be the two gawky girls, brains, teachers' pets, goody-goods, at the back of the line, perfectly content to be with each other and talk and gossip. Mary L. had said: Good luck to you, but things will change. We won't be friends in the same way. She didn't say it in a mean tone, but it wasn't friendly either: You'll have other eggs to fry; you're shaking your head no, but if you didn't, why are you going? You don't know what it is but you're going anyways; you're making a decision; you've decided to go against this—she was pointing to the long line of girls in their white robes holding a single rose each, and the nuns in front with no roses, and the parents on the sides in Sunday dresses and sport shirts, the bishop in the front, the long hot afternoon in the stifling church with lemonade and cookies on the rectory lawn. It's not so bad, Anne Kane was starting to say, but the procession had started and Mary Conley had that deaf look on her face with her lips drawn into a pencil line.

SEVEN LAST WORDS

It's quiet. The last train left, came and left a while ago although I didn't see, not from here, and there aren't trains for them to leave a silence as easy as this. There's quiet, but a wind through the olives and olivets, a wind over the ground, in and around the men who stand around me; you've seen them, bulky bodies and rude garments, red flat robes and hair falling on the shoulder; everything is tied with ropes. It's quiet, but this is not saying no one is shrieking, or weeping, turning a yellow eye up to the chalky sky, ready to turn, as the sky always is at this moment, ready to turn violet to black, those sullen tints.

This is me in my beholding, my full self. If I or my father am a full imagining hole, a hot center with a spiraling wire, then what are you, all the dead stars, the motes, the empty wood houses, the feet padding on these rocks round and round? To say the one, is it to say the other? This is what you have always thought, but what I have always thought is a fullness entails an annihilation. To say one is to forget what you could be, to leave you unannounced with no memory to lift you from those other formless ideas. To say me is to say nothing else and this is what you always say, always thoughtless.

I have one hat and this hat of pain is my reminder that I have a contracting flesh and one full of doubt. This hat has a humorous design and is full of the pricks of conscience, the inwits, and the humor of a hat worn for study, for sorrow, for a kind of human science, even as you have your hats and some covering your eyes and down over the lips. You've never seen me laugh but I have a laugh that is like a curtain of birds, a flowering stick, and I have laughed these many times when you would not watch.

And what would I have to eat? A carved and roasted bird, an unction, something sweet on a metal probe, or just this liquid you have made for me and I sip with my tongue so swollen and lips rounded with the patterned speech of pathos. Am I a mirror or an ape? And if I eat, is this another animal in my throat? My agony is also yours.

There will be a brevity and a quietness. You think that this— I—will end but there burns in memory always this image, and

45

it will not be burned out or scorched from the face of this flat dirt. I doubt, like you, of an end.

There is something inside me enlarging, if an egg could grow, and I could travel my days again and kiss, soothe, tantalize, and re-form my favorite cadence with outstretched finger. There is something of life that I would love.

Father?

T was Christmas time, but Dr. Eagle had said don't go home. She didn't want to go home anyway (Don't force me to come home, she said on the phone to Marie, if I don't want to. *Don't* then, Marie said, but don't come home ever again. Maybe, Annie said, just Christmas and the day before. Marie said don't do us any favors. I said I'd come home Christmas and maybe the day before and the day after.), but she didn't want to stay where she was, in the dorm, not a nice place for Christmas. She was seeing her doctor every morning except weekends and he said again he didn't want her to go home and lose all that time, make a big gap, so she stayed, although everyone else went home. It was then, just a week before Christmas vacation that a new person she had met on the shuttle to the medical school asked her if she might be interested in housesitting. The roommates would be away (Alex flying to California for the holidays, Jill to New York); their house would be empty and convenient; plus, it would be a help to them if she would consider it.

She had met the new person by accident. Every day she climbed aboard the blue bus at eight, barely awake, and tried to arrange her thoughts and be ready to lie on the couch in Dr. Eagle's office and stare at the light fixtures. It was like examining your conscience before confession, although it wasn't enough to say the sins, you had to say *why* you were saying them and you had to be awake enough to remember them. "I know you," the person was saying; "I think you're in one of my classes." Miss Kane hated to show a tired, depressed face to a new person but wanted to take a look at this, so lifted up the head that had sunk to her chest and opened the eyes glued shut, pink and painful. This was a large, blonde girl with blue eyes and a round face. Over her wool coat was a pink and blue angora or mohair—Miss Kane didn't know which—shawl, wrapped around her neck and so bulky it covered part of her head. Over this shawl hung a heavy yellow braid. Sometimes Alex wore the hair in a braid—now, Miss Kane remembered her: chemistry class—sometimes she let it fly out like a thick hat; it was waist-length and wavy: each of the hairs was electric and chattered around the shawl. This, Miss Kane thought, was a fascinating girl.

Now Alex sat with her all the time, and had long ago stopped asking where she was going and why, and for how long and for what problems. Alex herself had a psychiatrist but was using the shuttle bus not to see him, but to take make-up courses in science for medical school. Everyone Miss Kane knew was going to medical school, although for now doing more interesting things. When she had arrived at Harvard, she wasn't going to medical school, or anywhere, but little by little she was planning to go. She started with a premedical course, a hard one, but not interesting; so after the hard one, she took an easy one and this was more like it. It was in the easy courses that you felt yourself really at Harvard. Alex, who talked a blue streak to and from the medical school, had taken no hard ones; in the easy ones, she had met the son of a Rockefeller, a Kennedy, a big South American, son of an industrial giant and always in a suit with yellow calfskin shoes, a Dupont, a young woman who lived in the Ritz Carlton for a dorm, a Hearst, a White Russian. . . . Miss Kane by now had been in the kind of course—she didn't need Alex to tell her about them—where the professor, 150 years old, rich and snooty, in an old baggy suit, asked you to meet him for tea and a snack at the Hong Kong, first talk your ear off, then sit on your side of the booth, or offer to put a Chinese appetizer right in your mouth, but Alex said that had never happened to her.

She was an early admission (they had sent, she told Miss Kane, a telegram to the house and to the apartment) to Harvard Med, even without this basic course in chemistry that she and Miss Kane were taking together, and Miss Kane trying to help her with because she took such bad notes. On the bus, Annie Kane had looked at a few pages of these. They were written in a beautiful rounded hand, fountain pen—she had seen it, gold with a surface of tiny squares, a very slim pen and kept in its own leather case with matching pencil and cartridges: fun to watch Alex take it out, uncap it, give it a little wipe with an old-fashioned penwiper, but by that time, Dr. Roskow was already into the first topic, maybe past it. He always listed the day's worth of topics on the board and called it his docket, then went through the topics one by one. He was an old man with a cheery voice and all he had to do was lecture on the docket to 200 students twice a week and he could go home; the little foreign section men were the ones who had to live day and night in the smelly old Mallinckrodt—no one ever let them out—and do the rest: talk to the students, grade the tests, and fail the ones who couldn't do the math: tears and hysterics, lawsuits, fathers coming up in chauffeured limousines from Wall Street and Washington. Dr. Roskow could remain, Miss Kane had watched him and noticed this, nice as pie, but maybe he *was* nice as pie.

Miss Kane felt bad for these section men. She had one of her own;

he wasn't foreign, but he was ordinary. He was so ordinary he wasn't able to see how ordinary she was, and everybody else could spot that right away. Mark W. Wood, Vermont, and always in a wool shirt and boots, was trying to push her ahead and into a harder course: a girl like you should be a doctor or a research scientist, he had said to her when he was threading through the sheets of problem sets, carefully done, but not always finished: this course is too elementary, why don't you take the course for majors? She was sick of this question. She was good in science, yes, but she didn't like it; she didn't *dis*like it; there was nothing to think about all those hours in the cold, damp lab while something was heating up or melting down, then measured and thrown away. It was like being in prison and making tires. *He* liked science; you could tell he didn't mind all those hours spent in the lab when he could be out strolling around the square looking in windows; he like the lab and the smells, but he wasn't happy either. He wanted to be a doctor too, but they wouldn't let him into medical school. Why?

She was sitting in his little basement office right outside a big lab, smelled like an outhouse in a picnic grove, and he was trying to eat his lunch. "I don't know why," he said. "I like your hat." Miss Kane was wearing a striped hat from France, found in the laundry room at Crowninshield Hall: she had also found a serape there, a little ripped, but straight from Mexico—she wore it everywhere, just like everyone else. Miss Kane took the hat off. He didn't know, spending all his time in the lab and living in a cheap apartment, Central Square, that this hat was just one thing; you needed all the other things to go with it; and all the other things on her and in her face were not those things, they went against it; but he took it on faith, or on the hat, that he was talking—she could see he did—to a genuine Cliffie. Only someone like this, so naïve, would do it.

Why? Tell me why.

I don't know. It might be because I have a doctorate in chemistry, they don't think I'm serious.

Get out.

Mark Wood did not want to talk about this subject. When will *you* go?

Anne Kane did not want to talk about it either.

He picked up the striped hat. Why are you thinking about going to medical school, tell me? You don't seem like the type. Can't you think of something better to do?

It's not that you aren't smart enough. He dropped the hat on the desk and picked up the sandwich. Anne Kane put the hat back on. She didn't like this. She'd never be a doctor if people thought of questions like this to ask. They weren't trying to be mean, but when they said that Anne Kane was not going to be a doctor because she didn't look like the type, they were saying: your life won't ever be different that it is now. It was a compliment; they meant it as a compliment, but it wasn't a compliment. She liked the idea everybody hated: that a medical school took its college graduates, each different and interesting: plays, instruments, Heidegger, working for your congressman, crew, Hasty Pudding, fly-fishing, junior year in Florence, and made them more alike. People criticized this, but what was wrong with it? Doctors were happy. They had the same amount of money to spend, they talked alike. They looked down their noses at anything nonmedical; they weren't distracted or afraid that somewhere else—Lehman Hall, Agassiz Theater, Adams House, Brattle Street, the old yard, the boat house, Design-Research, the French cafés, the bars and tea houses, the common rooms, the book stores—something better was going on and they were missing it. Something had to happen to you like this, or you just went along—like she did—from place to place, and some of these places *very* different, being yourself.

➤ Alex Canfield was not smart in science. After a while, Miss K. just gave the girl her notepad and let her copy out a week's worth of notes. "You just listen to Dr. Roskow," she said, "and I'll take the notes." This was working fine, except that Alex had fallen behind in her copying and had, she explained, to hang on to Anne's notepad, or else she just forgot to bring it back, so Annie Kane started taking notes on looseleaf paper, and passed the sheets to Alex after the class. "We can study together," Alex said one day when she was filing a set of notes into her leather schoolbag, "in the end." The midterm, Dr. Roskow had said, was one week away, and what Miss K. didn't know was Alex wasn't keeping the notes: she discarded the notes once she had copied them into her own notepad. Miss K. discovered this one day on the bus. She had a good memory, she told Alex, so if the girl would just return the notepad, she could keep all the loose notes, Miss K. would just try to remember what Dr. Roskow had been saying. "You're going to be upset with me," Alex said, turning her face away and looking out the window. "No, I'm not," Miss K. said, as they jounced along in the blue schoolbus, holding on to the front seat. "Yes, you are. You have a right to be."

Her room, she started out saying, was a pigpen—notes, clothes, books, pads, old letters, stuffed animals on the floor, cracker boxes, empty bottles, old tissues—a mess, and in a depression because couldn't get any work done at all and had a fight with the boyfriend, a professor from California, who called every night. Miss K. knew all about this boyfriend, Jackson O. Spires, because Alex had shown her one of his letters, then showed her every letter: he's obscene, she had said, with a grin on her face.

"He writes me—don't mention this to anyone—pornographic letters. He says he can't help it."

"You're so interested," the girl said, a day later, "I thought I'd let you see." They were on stationery from the University of California, typed, but the girl was right: some of what he was talking about Miss Kane hadn't even heard of. She was surprised a girl like Alex, such beautiful clothes and perfect English, would want to get a letter like this.

"Anyway," the girl was saying, "I broke up with Jacks on the phone. I called him right back, but I was still upset, and I told you my room was a mess? It was. I had—you're not going to believe this— just eaten—I'm almost ashamed to tell you—a whole Sara Lee Danish, and not just a piece, a whole cake; I didn't even heat it up; it was half frozen; *you* know what I'm talking about.

"Well, I was simply disgusted with myself. Who wouldn't be? Suddenly," Alex was looking out the window, "I was just lying there on my bed, crying, the bed was full of crumbs; my stomach hurt, plus I was getting my period [Miss Kane wanted to laugh, but no.] and then the phone rang. It was my *mother*. What a time to call. You know how well I'm getting along with my mother now; we're like best friends. Well, that's something new; usually, I despise her and she despises me just as much; I think she's jealous. Sometime I'll tell you some of the things she does to my father, the kind of selfish bitchy things she's famous for, no one would believe it. But I was crying on the phone and must have been crying like that for an hour. It was pathetic.

"She didn't know what to say to me. There was nothing to say. Finally, she said to me: take some money—she would reimburse me—and get on the subway to Boston, go to Lord and Taylor's or Bonwit's and buy myself a nice new sweater, the best sweater I could find—as if *that* would help me.

"Well, I did it, but not that minute. I collect sweaters—but *you* know that." Alex had taken a quick look at Miss Kane, then out the window again; there was nothing to look at out there.

"I felt a little better; I stopped crying, and took a good look at my room . . . "

Alex Canfield had in a frenzy cleaned this room; it made her feel good to do it. It was a fit of cleanliness; everything in order. "You should have seen me," the girl said, grinning at Miss Kane, then out the window. "I was, in your terminology, a ball of fire."

It was this ball of fire that had scooped up all of Miss Kane's old notes and the notebook: they were all over the room, "and don't forget," the girl said, "some of them were on single sheets; they weren't all in one place; if they had been, it never would have happened," and threw them away. She was sorry now. Then, she didn't know what she was doing. "I shoved it all into two shopping bags and took them out to the trash, a freezing cold day and raining, and believe me, I thought of going back out there, even though it was already night, but I didn't think I'd be able to find them in the dark.

"Yell at me, if you want to; I deserve it; I threw away your property."

Miss K. didn't know what to say. Alex Canfield said she went right upstairs and called her psychiatrist to make an emergency appointment. "I explained it all to Dr. Fagan—I mentioned you—and he had a theory of his own that I was competing with you for something; he didn't go so far as to say I wanted to make sure you couldn't study for the chemistry test, but he *did* say, and I thought you might be interested in this, that we must be very similar in some ways, like sisters, and that's where all the rivalry comes from. I thought you'd like that. I thought it was very interesting.

"Anyway, as you can see, I won't be able to study either. I never finished copying all you gave me, you know." She turned to Miss Kane; "We're in this together, see what I mean?"

Miss Kane didn't know what to say; she didn't want to say the wrong thing. The girl had talked about her to her psychiatrist; that was nice, and a compliment, but she was scared not to have the notes, good memory or not.

"We'll study together," Alex said; "you can borrow my notes whenever you want." Miss Kane wanted to talk; she was not as mad as Alex thought she was; she wasn't mad at all. Alex C. put her arm through Miss K.'s arm; "You won't be mad at me for a long time, will you? I couldn't stand that. I like you too much. I *do*. You always make me feel better."

Miss Kane didn't have time to study for the test anyway, so it didn't matter, notes or no notes. She got a C– when Mark Wood made a curve of the grades. He wrote a note on her test: I'm surprised. I was sure you knew this material. Come and see me.

She didn't know this material; she might have known it, but she didn't. She hadn't cracked, as her mother would say, book one. She had, her father would say, other eggs to fry.

❧ When they got to Cambridge, they skipped Dr. Roskow's class and had a sundae instead, Alex's treat. It was fun. Alex explained that none of what she said on the bus had really happened. She had just discarded the notes. "I know this doesn't make sense, Anne; I don't understand it either, but I didn't want you to be mad at me. I want you," and there were tears in her eyes, "to try and understand me."

It was shortly after this test (Alex Canfield passed also, by the skin of her teeth, but she didn't have to worry too much, she told Miss K., because there was still time to make an A on the final and she knew she could "if you keep helping me." But Miss K. wasn't going to be as much of a help now because she wasn't going to all the classes and even when she went, she wasn't paying attention; Alex Canfield must have noticed this, for she never asked for notes again, even though Miss Kane had bought a fresh notebook: it said HARVARD on it, but it was almost empty) that Dr. Eagle told her not to go home for Christmas, to stay nearby and come to see him every day during the vacation. She explained this to Alex on the bus and that was when she got a nice surprise. Alex and her two roommates, Elizabeth and Jill—Alex was always talking about them: history and literature and art history, they were very interesting girls; Annie Kane had spotted them one day, with Alex, in the Design Research store: they were looking at dresses and material for dresses. Annie Kane had wandered into this store, all windows and bright colors but everything expensive, and caught sight of the three girls but was too embarrassed to say hi to Alex; what if Alex ignored her while she was with her cronies? This had happened before, so Annie Kane was a little more careful about going up to people she knew to say hi: they were looking at these dresses which were cotton and full and had one big design on them in a bright color; Annie had seen them before; they were very recognizable and everyone liked them around here. In fact, one of Alex's friends had one of these dresses on and was looking for another one. Their voices were very sweet as they discussed the dresses: Annie Kane had turned her back so she could listen and not be seen. They sounded so cheerful and comfortable with each other, yet also smart and important: like most of the people here, they pronounced their words carefully and always added an interesting word to each ordinary sentence. They never used slang and they never made any mistakes in grammar while they talked. They didn't have ordinary voices, all flat and lifeless, or hard and jabbing; they had voices that sounded like singing, each one sounding different, and they always sounded very good together. After a while, out of the corner of her eye, Annie could see one of the girls take a white shopping bag with DR on it, and all three left the dress counter; now the voices were higher and Annie heard that Elizabeth was off to meet a boy, "Daniel" they called him, at the Village Blacksmith, a teashop right next door; he was, Annie heard because Alex was telling Jill in a very bright voice, editor of the *Advocate* and the son of the New York attorney general, and Elizabeth had met him in Robert Lowell's (Annie Kane knew this name) class, and he was a problem. They were discussing in just what ways and just what she should do, when Miss K. couldn't hear them anymore. They were going to walk her over there, the two of them, Annie figured, to keep her spirits up with advice and smart thoughts on how to be a know-it-all: film, famous people, important teachers, Christmas parties, vacations, and skiing; Miss K. had heard this advice before, but it was a little too late for her to apply it to herself because people already knew she didn't know anything—were going home for Christmas and would Anne be interested in house-sitting their apartment? Annie Kane said yes before she even thought a minute if she wanted to. It's true, the apartment was closer to Dr. Eagle—it was then she found out that Ralph, as they called him, had another patient, and she was sure, looking back, that Jill Blumenthal found out that night—and to the museum and she could get away from school and the square and have "some space." Alex invited her to come over one night for supper, just something small, and she could see the apartment and where the plants were and what things the housemates wanted her especially to keep an eye on.

* Anne Kane, junior honors, pre-medical/undeclared, twenty years old, moved into the apartment on a snowy day, December 22. She took one suitcase and one book, *The Magic Mountain*, because her new boyfriend had recommended it and it was a thick book and would last a week or two when there'd be nothing else to do. She got

on the subway and walked to the double street with a little park in the middle till she came to Alex, Jill, and Elizabeth's brownstone and unlocked the green door to their first-floor apartment. It was very quiet. She carried her suitcase and book into the kitchen where there was a bowl of apples on the table, soft ones because they had been left out, but still smelled nice. The kitchen was tiny, filled with cooking things, spices, ingredients, and cookbooks—all the shelves were lined with flours, sugars, honey, syrups, teas, and big empty jars. In the refrigerator were more ingredients for cooking and the dregs of a bottle of French wine. Annie Kane put her book on the table; it had a black cover, and her suitcase on the floor. She looked in each of the bedrooms, all very small and filled with books and clothes. There was hardly any room to move, and there was no room anywhere to put anything, so she left her suitcase in the hallway and later moved it to the bathroom. When she had looked over everything and opened every drawer and closet, there was nothing to do, so she lay down on Alex's narrow bed with the quilt on it and started reading; but it was too cold to read; the wind was coming right off the street and into the rattly window, so she moved to one of the other bedrooms, then to the kitchen, which was warm because it had no windows. She sat at the little table with the book. Time was going very slowly and there was nothing special to do till tomorrow at nine o'clock when she'd walk to the hospital to visit Dr. Eagle. He'd be there; he was only taking the day off for Christmas; he'd be there before and after with a day full of appointments. It was starting to get dark and Annie Kane had forgotten she was supposed to go shopping; they had told her that night at supper where the supermarket was, but now she wasn't that sure. She wrapped up in extra sweaters, a hat she found in the hallway and went into a blast of cold. There was nobody on the street. She walked around the block to the main street and marched five blocks to a lighted area and there was the market. It was open.

In the handbasket she put gum, apples, raisins, shredded wheat, Oreos, bananas, milk and a frozen chicken pie. This seemed like a lot of food, but near the end she added a pint of strawberry ice milk and two oranges. This was heavy and she walked home slowly, the cold was unbearable and she had to sit on the radiator in Alex's room for fifteen minutes to stop shivering. This was not a very warm house and nothing to do but wear all the clothes she could find. She put the groceries, the whole unemptied bag, into the refrigerator and lay down on the bed in Jill's room, a smaller room, but a little warmer. She had forgotten the book, so she just lay there with her eyes open in the dark.

The phone was ringing. She heard it but was in the middle of a long, complicated thought, trying to get to the point of it, and feeling herself getting sadder and sadder as she worked toward it; it was the story of the last three months and it wasn't a good story. Why?—she got up to cover her feet and to stuff part of the bedspread along the bottom of the window; flopped back on the bed with an arm across her eyes—when everything here was so good, were things so bad? This was the mystery of it.

She loved this place, Harvard, better than any place she had ever been in her life: it was pretty, there were wonderful places to sit and read or sit and look out the window, she had friends who could do everything and had done everything: they were dramatic and musical, smart and stuck-up; they weren't afraid of anything, their parents weren't afraid of anything. They had two sets of clothes— messy, black clothes, ordinary clothes for school—some of these clothes from the Army-Navy Surplus store; and the other set of clothes for when they would take a cab to Logan and get on an airplane in a coat with a big fur collar and a special dress and appointment with a Boston hairdresser. They had plans for each vacation and their parents were anxious to see them—with prospects for parties and dinners and visits—even if it was just to criticize, just to change their ways. She loved these people. She knew she would love them right from the beginning when her boyfriend, her old boyfriend, dropped her off and dropped her suitcases off at Crowninshield Hall, and her room, a room all by herself, was crammed with trunks marked: Nell F. Beechcroft, H. F. Beechcroft, or Helen Fitzroy Beechcroft, 4 Nobby Lane, Wenham, Mass., and Annie sat on the bed, just a twin bed, metal, hideous and unmade, while Mr. Beechcroft and Nell's brother, Christopher Beechcroft, and Nell's little sister, Sarah Beechcroft—Annie tried to help them, but no, they wouldn't hear of it—filed in to drag out the trunks. "Sorry, wrong room." Nell never came into the room. She was way down the hall unpacking the trunks. They were beautiful trunks, all wood or all black metal and full of things. When the trunks and hatboxes—were those hatboxes?—were gone, Annie Kane looked out the window—it was a pretty window with small panes and a line of cars emptying out suitcases and trunks and footlockers and racks of dresses, schoolbags, sewing machines and dolls, rockers and wicker baskets and flowers. It was very quiet and serious compared to the last school. No one was screaming or laughing. The mothers and fathers were friendlier, at least that first day, and very businesslike, anxious to get the task done and their daughters anxious, too, to get it all started and get the parents and brothers out and away. Annie Kane, who had left her door open a little, kept hearing these beautiful clear voices rising so fast and falling so delicately on the subject of the summer vacation just past. People did some very nice things. One girl, Sasha, summered at Pea Town, another at Mount Desert Island. Where these were, Annie didn't know: up Maine or maybe in Florida. Another girl, with a very flat voice and the name of Martha said she went to a play every single night; it sounded like a punishment but Miss Kane heard that story again at dinner, when a big pack of them let her have dinner with them and talked to her a little at the round wooden table. This Martha, whose father taught mathematics at Columbia University—Miss Kane was not impressed by the fathers anymore; everyone's father did something great and in a great place and in fact, she was a little snobbier after a couple of weeks and knew the really great places from the places that were just good and okay. Sometimes these daughters had to make up things: one father was a spy, another a personal friend of John Kennedy and a relation of Winston Churchhill, plus an opera singer, Miss Kane had heard some beauts, as they used to say, but she was getting a little better at detecting a story—had spent the summer by herself in London.

Martha was a fat girl with a beautiful black cape she wore everywhere. She had a set of friends and these friends made an attempt to include the new student, third floor, from some girls' college on the South Shore nobody had ever heard of, into their group: Lane, a tall, brown-haired girl with a long face, from Oregon; Barbara, a short girl from Long Island; and Sidney, a deaconess (that's all Miss Kane knew) from New Haven, Connecticut. These were very strange girls and not very friendly. Annie followed them one night after dinner—a horrible dinner, always half-cooked and tasteless, although Annie wasn't that picky about food. Some of the students didn't eat the cooked food at all, she had noticed. Instead they made a pile of lettuce and put a pile of cottage cheese on top of it and covered it all with salad dressing. Or else they just made a big pool of soupy unflavored yogurt. At first, Annie didn't know quite what this bowl, next to the cottage cheese, was full of: so strange and lumpy it looked, until she heard someone call it yogurt and then get up and spoon a big pile of it into a cereal bowl, then four tablespoons of sticky strawberry preserves sunk in the middle. Annie decided not to try this just yet—into the common room to meet Professor John R. Marchplace, art historian. There was a little card at dinner saying he would have after-dinner coffee in Crowninshield Hall and speak with students from the large lecture course, Fine Arts 10, because Radcliffe believed in personal exchange between the young ladies and their professors, that's what somebody had said.

Professor Marchplace was tall with a beard and was smoking a pipe. They had him sitting in a green armchair and a big fire with all the lamps lit, too, and a table with glasses and a few dark brown bottles, coffee and tea in silver urns, cups and saucers from the dining hall, teaspoons and napkins. Professor Marchplace, who was by himself, had a napkin on his knee and a cup balanced. In his other hand was the pipe and a tiny glass of the brown wine. Nobody was talking to him, but he didn't look nervous. Martha and her friends were the first to arrive and Martha, a professor's daughter, walked right over to him and stood next to his knee. She loved Fine Arts 10 and always sat in the same seat, sometimes Annie Kane sat next to her. Her favorite artist, she had told Miss Kane, was Vermeer. They had gotten to Vermeer just a couple of weeks ago, but Annie had already heard of him and even remembered a picture with blue in it from Art Appreciation, once a month. The nuns would pass out little postcards with black and white or colored pictures of paintings in museums, mostly the famous ones that everyone knew: *The Last Supper, Blue Boy, Strawberry Girl, Mona Lisa, Madonna of the Chair, The Sower*. First, they would look at the picture totally free, just a look to see it in its beauty and importance, without the words. There would be two or three minutes of silence while the children, in their uniform skirts and pants, 2 P.M. Friday afternoon, third week of the month, holding the cards, or laying them squarely on the desk, lips sealed, feet flat on the floor, with hot steam coming out of the radiators or fresh spring trees and mud coming through the open windows, looked. No matter how many times they looked at these pictures, or how many pictures they looked at—and they were all a little bit alike—no one in their class could ever figure out what the words would say; it was always a surprise. No one ever won the special prize, a postcard or candy prize, for guessing what some of the words would say, or just one of the ideas about the pictures, that the nun would then dictate from her desk where the picture was also laid squarely in a place all bare and empty. The words were strange. They described in just the way this professor would describe what was in the painting that wasn't visible to the eye, like where the light was coming from—no matter how deeply Anne M. Kane, Grade 4, HSS, looked into the quiet picture, she could never see this pool of light, which would then be described in such a pretty way as if it were so much light; even after the description pointed to what part of the picture this fresh light was in, it never seemed like that much— or the fold in the drapery, the modeling of the figure, the arrangement of the forms: all these were interesting, but the pupils didn't know what they meant. It didn't matter. The description was copied out carefully in the art book, then the picture was put in the art book and held in there with black corners or silver corners, which you had to buy beforehand and which Anne M. Kane was always forgetting to bring in from home, if she could have found them at home, where they were always in a different place and sometimes lost. Picture on the left, dictation on the right, then the nun would swish by and check each one and make a comment. There was one Vermeer, the inside of a room with a blue pitcher on a table. Anne M. Kane liked this one; it was pretty to look at and very calm, but it didn't seem like a real room: it was just a picture and the nun read the lovely description and they copied it out.

And there he was again on the screen in the Fogg Lecture Hall, Vermeer, and the same room, but bigger, and now it looked much more like a room, and Martha said exactly where the picture was, how big it was and when Vermeer had painted it. It all seemed closer now; even the professor seemed close, although he was way up there on the stage. It was easy to come up with these same descriptions that seemed so hard and out of the blue in grade 4: the drapery, the fold, the light source, modeling, composition: all this was right there once they told you what words to use, and Anne Kane loved using these words. You could write the description without even looking at the picture and this was what many students did; but she liked making the trip on the subway to the MFA and getting in free as a Harvard student, traipsing over to this or that gallery where there'd already be a little pack of students from FA 10 standing in a semicircle about four feet from the picture, looking up, then looking down and making a little jotting in a notepad. Sometimes the girls would sit on the floor cross-legged and look up, then down. Nobody cheated or copied. There was no need to: you just looked and wrote the words you learned in the class from Professor Marchplace and the other professors. Now, they always knew what they were looking at: they could size a picture up, just the way they did in hourly exams: artist's name, picture name, date, museum or country of birth, type of picture, historical style, influences, and a little description in art history terms of what was in the square—first looked at one way, then another. They knew everything now and no conversation about art, no trip to a gallery would leave them at a loss for words. Annie Kane thought this was exactly the kind of course that was a help to you in getting along day by day in a place like this. She was wrong. It didn't help at all. The first time she got to use this handy knowledge was when she met an artist who painted realistic pictures of hell and was the grandson of a famous Jewish painter; used to be an intellectual until he couldn't stand the pretensions anymore, and wanted her to model maybe, but first come over and see the pictures he had already done; she said a few of these things you're supposed to say to lay the groundwork. They were standing in a small room in Boston, reeking of oil paint, looking at pictures leaned against the wall; in the other room was the wife of the artist and the baby son, both of them eating Campbell's tomato soup and the wife had even offered her some, but no thank you, and he said: how foolish you sound, you don't know how to see, you're just parroting the garbage you pick up at Harvard and the Harvard art history department; I hear exactly what they think and don't you think I already *know* that. He stopped talking.

I might be willing to take the time to show you some things, but who knows, you might be too far gone to learn anything. He stopped talking again. Let's get out of here, he said; let's go for a drink somewhere. I've done enough for today. He left to go into the other room. Now, he was talking to his wife, if that woman *was* his wife. When he came back, Annie Kane said; shouldn't I go say goodbye? Hurry up, he said, and she went into the kitchen and the wife asked her again in a very soft voice if she wouldn't stay and have some soup with the baby, and she was starting to sit down when the artist stuck his head in the door: Don't get settled. Sarah, you'll get a chance to talk with Anne later. We'll be back and you two can become as friendly as you want to.

All this had already happened, and she was still in FA 10, a survey, just a student, but it wasn't the same. She didn't like that artist, Jesse his name was; he was mean to her, he was mean to his wife; he hated everyone. He was painting her in an ugly way, all yellow, but it didn't matter. Pretty soon it would be over and she wouldn't have to go there anymore and say hi to Sarah and the baby, then put on an old raggy dress and stand against the wall next to a fake red tree. It took a long time and he talked all the time. Sometimes the baby cried and Jesse would leave the apartment and Anne Kane would go with him. They'd go to Mike's Tavern on the corner and drink whiskey and beer. He'd drink whiskey, Anne Kane would drink a rum coke, the only drink she had ever had that tasted okay. Then she'd get on the subway and go home. Sometimes Jesse would try to tell her his feelings, how much he liked her and how important this was to him. She listened, but she didn't believe it. He kept saying it. She went three times, then never went back there again. The girls on her floor said he had come by and asked where she was. Don't tell him, she said.

It was much better, she was thinking, not to have any dates at all, but to stay with these girls and spend the evening in Crowninshield Hall with a professor, or even without one. No one else was coming, and Professor Marchplace had stood up to talk to Martha and Lane and the Deaconess. Anne Kane was standing a little behind them and listening to what they were saying. They were talking about travels, seeing the real pictures and the real buildings. What happens, the teacher was saying, is you see a picture of the picture, all flat and perfect and in a perfect light, immobilized on a screen or in a book. Then you see the real picture in a museum and it's not as clear or as big: no one has picked it out for you and set it in a context and forced you to concentrate your gaze. Professor Marchplace's gaze had traveled over Martha's left shoulder and onto Miss Kane's face, all droopy and dull with attention. This was a beautiful thing he was saying. They were in a perfect room and having the ideal conversation. But then, he said, taking a sip of his drink, you get used to the picture in the museum and you see it in an exciting way as a painting, as something somebody did. You can see the paint on the picture, the bumps and points of the brushstrokes, you can imagine the artist applying the paint, painting on the surface, you can imagine it half done, then scraped, then done again. You can imagine, he was saying as more students came in and stood in a loose group around him, how the artist didn't know at that point whether it was done or not. This was so exciting to hear. Someone asked a question and Professor Marchplace answered it. It distracted him, Miss K. could see that, and the discussion—the part of it that interested her—was over and he was back on travels again and a comparison of one artist to another, and sounding like an authority because that's the way the students sounded. The group got larger and Professor Marchplace broke away from it little by little until he was near the door, then slipped out. Anne Kane was sorry to see him go. That, she told

Martha, who was silent and by herself, is a nice man. Who? Martha said. Him. I know, Martha said. I didn't know he was so nice, Miss Kane said. She was drinking the third little glass of sweet wine. He's not *that* nice, Martha said. What? Don't idealize him, that's all. Miss Kane loved this piece of advice: don't idealize him. She stuck close to Martha the rest of the night. Martha wanted to sew her curtains so Miss Kane followed her up to her room, where the curtain material, a gold brocade, heavy and stiff, was laid out on the bed. It's a Florentine weave, Martha said, sitting behind her sewing machine. Miss K. sat while the girl sewed long gold seams and long white seams. Martha's room was full of heavy things: a heavy dresser with a marble top, a brass umbrella stand and a huge fern in a bulky wood container. These were art objects some of them, Anne Kane knew that much, but she didn't exactly know how you came to acquire them so that they're just there in your room as part of the furniture. Martha had prints on the wall, all black and white or brown and white, and Miss Kane got up to look at them like she always did: they were dark, some were scenes, others were animals and fruit, some of the lines were very fine and some were scrawls and scribbles. Everything Martha had was old and now she was going to have these heavy gold curtains.

Martha, everyone knew and Miss Kane knew too, wanted to have a boyfriend. She was trying to have one: she tied a beautiful Paris scarf around her neck when she went to Fine Arts 10, and asked Miss Kane to look first before sitting next to her, to see if she wasn't already sitting next to someone and would like to be by herself, no girlfriends. She had fixed her room up like a palace and was trying to diet off the extra pounds that made, as anyone could see, a very pretty girl like Martha ordinary and drab, a tight block in her heavy cape with the beautiful floating scarf and a hard heavy face over it. So far, nothing was happening and Martha, Miss Kane could see, was bitter.

Miss Kane didn't know what to tell her, but it didn't matter because Martha didn't want to hear it, not from her, or maybe anyone. She wanted it to happen, she didn't want to discuss it or have to look too much like she was planning for it. She was a busy girl otherwise, with a complete schedule of hard courses, a set of friends and interests and things she could make for her room and more rooms of the future whether or not, Miss Kane thought, she gets married or stays an old maid.

Martha was quiet at her sewing machine, the material flowed over the top and fell down to the floor. Martha sewed up and down. She sewed a heavy white lining and then sewed the lining to the drape. The phone rang and she said call me later, I'm busy with my curtains and Anne Kane is here helping me; she hung up and went back to the sewing machine. This was very nice and Miss Kane sat in an old-fashioned upholstered chair, and watched. When Martha finished one whole curtain, the two girls went to the spa on Mass. Avenue and bought Cokes in bottles and a bag of Fritos. Martha also bought a bag of candy kisses and peanut butter kisses, a package of gum, the latest *Science Digest* magazine, a *TV Guide*, and a paperback novel, *Coffee, Tea Or Me*. She read a lot of paperback novels in between studying. On the way back to Crowninshield Hall, Martha outlined the facts about the six likely boys who had shown the most interest in her in Fine Arts 10, and where in the room they sat. She had researched them a little: they were evenly distributed among the houses and the concentrations, they were mostly from Protestant backgrounds, but one was Jewish and another was Indian, but not too Indian, and mostly from the East Coast with one exception from Chicago. Most everyone they knew wanted to go to medical school and the majority of these boys wanted to go to medical school, too. This was all right: it would give them time, Martha had said, to grow up. Miss Kane laughed. Martha was already talking of their points and appeal: some of them sounded so attractive when Martha would begin to talk about them. Miss K. had begged her to point them out so she could see how the descriptions applied.

One boy she had described only in terms of his neck. She loved boys' necks and this boy had a good one, strong but slim and set on the shoulders like a swan's neck, and shoulders like beautiful wings with just the lightest of downs, a silky down but very masculine. Miss Kane drew a breath when she heard this, and the tone of it. Martha would work her descriptions down the body and then up to the head, and by then Miss Kane could see the picture and would long to see the boy. Only once, though, had this happened.

Walking home from school, the way they always walked, through the law school, across Mass. Avenue, up Garden Street, Martha had worked on a magnificent, ultra-slender pianist from the Chicago suburbs, Leverett House, history and philosophy, pre-med, son of a manufacturer, accepted at Harvard and Hopkins Medical School, early admissions. She started—Miss Kane's eyes rolled back in her head—with the base of the spine, a declivity in the torso and source of extreme flexibility and suppleness. She put her hand on this, a simple flat hand with an onyx and diamond ring, her grandmother's school ring, and worked it up the back, cupping the hand to demonstrate on the air the careful hard curves of the back and narrow but perfect hips, high shoulders and strong thighs. Then she turned him around in the air and started with the front of him, ending with his head and feet, and only a brief digression onto the clothes and the fit of the clothes. Miss Kane had a perfect picture of this angel and kept it in mind, thinking about it at odd times of the day and at night, starting where Martha had started with the low point of the backbone until she felt she knew him.

Then Martha pointed him out. Professor Marchplace was talking about Tintoretto, whom Martha called Tintoret because Henry James did, or somebody did, and the picture was extremely complicated in brilliant colors when suddenly there was the boy from Chicago, and the most ordinary boy Miss Kane had ever seen in her life, perfectly insipid, as Alex would say with a hiss, not at all like the description. She turned to Martha to show her surprise, but Martha would not see it. She ignored it and never spoke of this one again, but there were others, and she continued to speak of them. By then, Miss Kane herself had become interested in this boy, Albert Edgar Rosenthal; there was a sign up in the Crowninshield dining hall about a piano recital by A. E. Rosenthal, Leverett House, and a program attached to it. Liszt, Scriabin, and Beethoven, and Miss Kane wrote the date on the back of a school pad, then went to the concert when the day arrived.

It was in a senior common room packed with people and the thin, pale boy was dressed in a narrow blue suit. His hands were as thin as skeleton hands, thin shoulders and back, but he could strike the keys with a power that was exciting to listen to, and Miss Kane stayed till the end and even longer, edging toward the front of the room where he was standing surrounded by some boys who lived in his hall, or went to the same organic chemistry lab, which they were talking about.

They were all musicians, Miss Kane figured, because they knew the music he played and were questioning him about it: why did he do this, and why did he do that; some of them were complimenting him. Miss Kane stood in a line to shake his hand and his hand was pink and moist with no force in it at all. He barely looked at her. She said: that was a beautiful concert you gave; you played like an angel. She didn't know she was going to say all this, but it was a good thing to say, not as dumb as it sounded. One of his friends repeated it to him and he laughed, but he liked it because he kept holding her hand, shaking it every once in a while, a hard shake. They were going to talk, she could tell, but his friends were collecting themselves to bring him to Boston, Lochober's, she heard, for dinner: no ladies could eat there, not that she wanted to go. What's your name? Do you mind my asking? he said, as he was closing up the piano and had his back to them. My name? I've seen you before; we're in a class together. But here they all were, and she didn't want to say her name. She said something, but so mumbly nobody could hear it. What?

☙ She didn't tell Martha about this but Martha had long since lost interest in this one; she didn't even go to the recital, although she had read the notice with Miss Kane and had nothing special to do that night. Martha didn't like going back to the square once the day was over; it was enough to walk it once a day, and plenty at night to keep her busy. Lane had a new project of buying all the nineteenth-century French and German operas and listening to them with copies of the libretti (libretti, Miss Kane remembered that word: libretti) from the music library. Martha, who had studied clarinet and voice, liked doing this, so every night Lane, a violinist in high school, and the Deaconess, conducted the youth symphony, made a pot of Oolong tea, loose tea in a pretty light-blue teapot, and got some fancy cookies from Sage's, or ice cream from the spa, and they would listen to a full opera in Lane's room. This was better, Martha told Miss Kane, more professional, a better style of music, more interesting, no amateurs, and don't have to go out and get into a cab and drive into Boston on a freezing cold night, rub elbows with jerks. Miss Kane tried it one time. They invited her and she brought a book along, Erik Erikson—everyone said it was beautifully written, but she didn't like it at all, too flowery, but had to read it anyway for a course, Soc Rel 51 (she had changed her major again, third major. She'd be lucky if she ever graduated and had two related courses to put together on her transcript), "Adolescence," taught by a big fat man who liked students and was the most popular teacher because everyone got an A and the section men were known to do psychotherapy if you asked them, or smoke dope, and go to the movies with the whole section, a nice course. Miss Kane got into it right away when she heard how special it was, and listened as this teacher repeated himself every single class, just the way the nuns did; he had three subjects: Margaret Mead, David Riesman, and Erik Erikson, and he talked about them, one book for each, and what they were like as people; he had met them all: they were all his friends. He was easy to listen to: Coming of Age in Samoa; The Lonely Crowd; Youth, Identity, and Crisis; The Lonely Crowd; Coming of Age in Samoa; Youth, Identity, and Crisis; The Lonely Crowd; Young Man Luther; Blackberry Winter; Coming of Age in Samoa; Presentation of Self in Everyday Life; Harry Stack Sullivan; Youth, Identity, and Crisis; this is what you had to remember, and hardly anyone came to class: you didn't have to; he was happy anyway—because she couldn't read music. It was fun to listen to: "Trovatore," they said, but it went on for a very long time and there was a danger, if you listened to things like this, that something would change and you wouldn't be normal anymore, but drink tea and walk to the square only for classes, spend the rest of the time in a bathrobe looking through auction catalogues and taking hard math courses, being fat, highbrow, and perfectly content.

But she didn't have to worry: it would never happen to her, Annie Kane. She stayed exactly the same no matter what happened. And things had happened: she was not studying for any of her courses, she had no more plans for the future. She was all alone because she had spent too much time, like Martha, trying to get a boyfriend and pin him down, but she had spent even more time, and while Martha stayed home in Crowninshield Hall and played her clarinet, fixed up her room and studied to get senior honors, ate dinner and gained twenty-five pounds in the dining hall with Lane and the Deaconess, met professors for sherry, sewed and knitted and made brass rubbings, did translations of Italian poems and went to church every Sunday, sang in the Radcliffe Chorale Society and had a job as a docent at the Fogg, plus was going to Europe to help restore the paintings drowned in the Venice flood; Miss Kane, or Kane as she now thought of herself, Kane, a zero, a failure at everything before she was a success at even the most measly thing, had done nothing but gain boyfriends and then lose them—and she wasn't even done yet; she still had one, gone away but coming back and so what? So what! She grinned with a thousand gleaming teeth. He was off on a vacation, Miles Max, but coming back—.

The room was so cold, her breath was a silvery smoke above the bed. That was the phone, someone was calling, or calling them and didn't even know they were away. "This is Deborah Newhauser, is that you, Anne Marie?" There was a Christmas party—not people from school, but friends of Deborah's, interesting people, artists, writers, a newspaperman, and older people, friends of the family, and Deborah knew she was in town alone and might like to come; would she?

Kane got off the phone. Yes, she had been busy in the boyfriend department, but what else had she done? Nothing. All she had done—it was dark outside and cold, too dark, too cold to go anywhere—since coming here in September—but she was also a little afraid of staying alone in this apartment—was what? Change majors and be analyzed. No, change majors and win a *scholarship* to be analyzed and imagine how nuts you'd have to be to get one of those. This outing, at least, would be a way out of spending the next few hours thinking about this. She lay on the bed. Time went by; it was late and now later. It was almost too late. The phone rang. Deborah said, if you haven't left yet, I'll come and pick you up. Where do you live? Kane wanted to say: I'm not coming. Sorry. Don't come and get me. Instead she said, okay, right off Huntington Avenue. She got back on the bed, this time into it: she was scared to go. She didn't have anything to say. She wasn't an interesting person. She was too nervous and upset. It was okay to stay home and read *The Magic Mountain* but she didn't want people looking at her right now, inquiring into her business: she had no business. If I were smart, Anne Marie Kane, I'd be dead, she said in a choked voice, a voice that didn't sound human.

A My name is Alice, my husband's name is Al. In the bed she started to cry. We come from Alabama and we eat apples. Crying hard, B my name is Barbara, my husband's name is Bob. She stopped, got up, washed her face with freezing cold water, poured the old French wine into a juice glass, drank it, found a pack of cigarettes, Chesterfields, in a drawer and smoked two in a row, put the dishtowel under the tap and wrapped it around her head, drank more of the wine—it stunk, all sour and grainy: why were they keeping it?—ironed a blue wool jumper she had sewed herself, perfectly square, simple and homely but the only thing she had packed that wasn't dungarees, play clothes, or too dirty; white blouse, red cardigan sweater, stockings and pumps, perfectly hideous—no one needed to tell her how hideous it was; she knew already. The ironing was not a good job, the sweater was missing a button and the ribbon under the buttons was not too clean, there was a run in her stockings and her shoes were flat. She went to the bathroom mirror: now *there* was a wreck of a face, all tired and sad and puffy; the hair, wet from the towel, was matted down and the eyes, red and strained. This was no good, but there was no time to make it better. Plus, it didn't matter.

DREAM DATE

To start with (on this hot summer day), the desirable boy up the street is out on the sidewalk in a set of clean laundry, while yourself—well, perhaps you'll stay out of it this time, stay home where you belong, rubbing the tape of the player piano between your lips to feel the bumps.

Or, he has a sailor hat on. You could put yourself a sailor hat and like a sailor speed up to his house and speed back letting him see what you have that's like he has.

Mother is in the kitchen waiting, perhaps, for the fruits of these experiments and for further evidence of what you can do. She, too, sees through her window the clothespin standing on its prongs and the small hat up there at the Conneally's. She also notes the white of his house, the blue of his sky and the kind of element that those Conneallys have always seemed to live in and up to you to open a tiny door between and let a little of it come down here, let her fill her fat lungs, she of whom the word fat wouldn't begin to describe, even by comparison with you, the sense to someone like him.

At what point you, the old mathematician, ask yourself, could you plot from here, the domain, to there: the white, the blue, the youth, the range? Can you be sure of leaving here, going there, getting him, coming back, in this universe of laws and materials dominated by laws, answer me, in an ellipse or a simple straight line doubled back? Would he be on your back? Could you start anywhere in the house and arrive, or can it be missed by a few degrees here and so much larger at the other end, fanning out— the brown dot—into the water right up to your maggot's neck, or back to the city on the other side, and him still standing there in his beautiful drapes and seaside frame.

How sad I am for your prospects and the sadness of your mother's prospects.

T was a nice sunny day. Alex was making a plum torte and Jill was in her room listening to Richie Havens, a familiar voice. They were doctors, or nearly; Jill, a resident at Children's Hospital and Alex, finishing a rotation in psychiatry and planning to go ahead and be an analyst later. The house was very clean and had been scrubbed and polished, all the floors were washed and waxed. There was a bowl of flowers on the kitchen table and a basket of dried flowers in the double living room. Alex had set a plain crystal punchbowl in the bay window on a gate-leg table. The punchbowl was filled with dry white wine and strawberries were floating in it. Around the punchbowl were different-sized wine glasses and a bottle of sherry and port with smaller glasses. Jill had moved her desk to the living room and covered it with an ironed sheet. On it were the cakes and breads they had been baking since last Saturday, and the cheeses and fruits Alex had bought yesterday morning in an early trip to Haymarket. At the far end of the table were teapots and a coffee urn, borrowed from the medical school dining hall. The coffee was not brewed yet and the pots stood empty. Alex had displayed them to get the balance of the table, and Jill had checked the effect. Things were perfect and on time.

The last cake was unmolded and placed on a flowered plate and a spot found for it on the crowded desk, and still a half hour before the earliest possible arrival. Alex's eyes darted, as she passed, into Jill's room. She was still in her bathrobe sitting on the bed reading a magazine and waiting for her electric curlers to heat up. Alex would like to know what she planned to wear, and arrange her own outfit accordingly, but no: Jill would be slow and ever so careful.

At 11:30, an hour later, the room was filled with spring sunshine, a Sunday, the fens still brown and gray and even a little snow on the ground but definitely warmer and sweet smelling; also filled with twenty young men and young women, not all doctors; Alex had insisted on variety, a mix, and they still had a few artist friends, a critic, a graduate student in English literature, and their former housemate who did very interesting work, Alex was telling Bob Brown, a neurologist at Peter Bent Brigham, at a mental health center somewhere in Boston. Who is she? Bob said, turning away from the stunning Alex in a long-sleeved, thin, navy-blue sheath, the narrowest column, reaching to her ankles with "patent-leather open-toed, slingback pumps" and her hair, freshly washed and dried in tiny braids so it stood out hair by hair like a golden furry cape over the shoulders and down the back, who was herself turning away and toward Kane, who had just knocked and been let in by someone she didn't know. Kane had never seen the hair like this before, so full and wiry and making the girl's head huge and full of sunlight and bristles.

"Here she is. Anne, meet Dr. Brown. Bob, Anne Kane Frazier. You two are interested in a lot of the same things. Anne did her under-graduate work at Harvard in psychology—that's right, isn't it? Bob was there, too, for a while, not the same time, I don't think, but I'm sure you know some of the same people, no?" Alex smiled, touched this doctor's elbow and Kane's elbow. "I'm so glad you had time to come," and turned away, walked toward the window and the group around the punchbowl, with the eyes of Kane and Brown on the long, lithe back in its sleek blue and the haystack of brilliant hair. Brown wanted to and tried to talk about the young Dr. Canfield, but Kane didn't let him. In a pink silky dress that looked at a distance like leather, and a smooth ponytail, a heavy handbag with books sticking out of it—he couldn't see the titles, but wasn't trying to see them especially—Kane asked the doctor a battery of questions, seeking brief empirical replies, which he could give, and gave: questions first about his specialty. She asked one question, a big general one, and then from his response, picked a second more focused question, and from the second answer, another, more closely aimed, until his face was flushed with however it had happened that he was talking about precisely the thing that interested him most on earth and was the hardest to say and could bring on, he was sure, a wave of derision because so new and untested, so idealistic and crazy. He talked. Kane was listening with an attention that had clamps and grips on it, and attached these grips to his growing idea and he saw it and felt the boost, went up, scurried up till he got as far as thinking alone, drifting, had ever taken him and so excited, he drenched his shirt with sweat and was taking off his wool jacket when Alex, who had seen a little of this, was at his elbow, and trying to lead him away, but first took the jacket from his arm and held it, with a wide, stretched smile and tilted head, for him to put his arms back into, which he did.

"I want to introduce both of you," Alex said, once the jacket was back on and Brown had wiped his forehead with a napkin he picked up from the cake table—Kane watched Alex watching this unthink-ing action, not the right action, no matter how hot and steamy, for a high tea, "so I'm going to have to break you up, and this interesting

conversation you were having—whatever were you talking about?"
(Canfield looked directly at Kane, who looked directly back; this
was not friendly, but Kane was certain she had not ruined the high
tea yet.) "Well, whatever it was, I can see how fascinated you were
and you can get back to it in a minute. Just let me introduce you . . ."
Dr. Canfield's voice trailed off as she led Brown by the hand to the
group by the punchbowl—three of these people were his colleagues
at Brigham, the other two were students of his and peers of Alex and
Jill's, but he went anyway.

Kane was alone in the large, sun-filled room only for a few minutes, during which she went to the cake table and poured herself a
cup of coffee, remembering these cups, thick and milky white. The
house looked the same; they had bought a few new pieces of furniture: a small black couch and a blue striped chair with an ottoman; it
looked more settled, even with the rug all rolled up and tucked away
somewhere and the glossy wood floors so exposed-looking, pretty
and just the way, Kane was thinking, a nice apartment full of student
doctors should look. At her elbow, pouring himself coffee and
adding a splash of bourbon that Alex had put out at the last minute
in a small decanter, was—lo and behold, as he said—Miles
Kasendorf.

Kane looked at Kasendorf pleasantly. And pleasantly, he looked
at Kane. The room was noisy with chatter and the overbrightness of
the sun, that sun coming across the naked floor and up a leg of the
table, making a yellow bullet hole in the decanter, also in the mirror.
"I thought," he said, sipping his coffee, "you might be here." Kane
opened her mouth to talk. Instead, Dr. Brown edged up in between
the K's and the K's had to wait. Miss Kane introduced Dr. Brown to
Mr. Kasendorf and Mr. Kasendorf to Dr. Brown, and said in a sentence how each was engaged in the world, a trim and polite defini-
tion with an undercoil or propeller of importance or glory. Dr.
Brown felt the creeping blood in his face from the propeller and Mr.
Kasendorf felt it, but it had not the same stir. For the rest of this
party or tea, the girl K rode with a full cape of Brown and Kasendorf,
who liked it. No works of Canfield could unfasten them; they were
there forever.

"Who is that guy?" Kasendorf said, when the doctor turned his
back to see who was behind him, tapping his shoulder. What guy?
Kane said, after Dr. Brown turned back to them to say nice to meet
you and walked away with the tapper, an older man, one of the main
doctors because soon mobbed by boys and girls and a burst of talk,

followed by a burst of silence while they waited for him to talk. "*That* guy." I don't know. I don't know him. "You were talking to him," Kasendorf said, reaching back to the table for the bourbon bottle, "weren't you?"

"Where . . . " Kasendorf started up again to Kane, but his glance was elsewhere, partly on the group around the doctor, partly flitting to this and that, taking in Jill's bedroom and the tall blue column standing in the bay window, holding the saucer of her coffee cup in the palm of her hand. "I haven't seen Canfield in an age," he said softly, "or Jill whatshername, the roommate; I never liked her anyway, too pushy, why the two of you were friends I never understood." He wasn't talking to anyone in particular; he was talking to himself.

"When are you getting married?" Kane Frazier said, all of a sudden, "or did you already tell me that before?"

K brought his eyes back to the person near him in the slippery pink with the heavy schoolbag. "What's that?" he said, bending his head toward her and folding his ear so he could hear better. "Oh," he let his ear flap back, "oh, I know what you're talking about. It's a long story." He was grinning. " Here, let me get you some more coffee." He took the full cup from her hand and with his own full cup turned, walked to the back of the table, said hi to a couple—some people who didn't seem to know him because they went right on with their conversation—put the cups down on the table, searched the room with his eyes, avoiding one spot near the table, caught the eye of Dr. Jill, saluted her from across the room, nodded quickly—eyes closed, lips in a smooth smile—to the figure in pink, and slipped from behind to in front, and in front to between, and between to through, and hi, nice to meet you, and before the stunning blue cylinder could stop his path—even though sighting him, through the quick word of a fleet Jill, only for the first time that day—a twirl of the doorknob and out the door. AKF moved to the bay window now empty to catch sight of the fleeing Kasendorf, and here was Dr. Brown again.

"Get lost," she felt like saying, "go peddle your papers," also "somewhere else. Go home, your mother's calling you. Scram, shoo!" Instead, and laughing, she presented the eager doctor with a pleasant but tight face and fifty-six white chiclets gleaming in rows on the inside of an even tighter smile. Such a smile even a tired doctor, with no gift for the psychological, could recognize.

And it was well for her because, although there was more to do and to say, there was no time to do it and say it because Kane had promised Mr. Frazier she'd be home in an hour, so they could take their daily silent walk and buy the food for their silent dinner and gather up the books for the silent evening and build up this still energy that was the life of the Fraziers, still new to each other; so she slid this doctor off her cape and sent it toward the copious hair helmet of Miss Canfield, and went out.

✤ Mr. Frazier had asked no questions about this Sunday morning social. He was aware of it. The alarm had gone off at 8:45 so she (she: he liked the sound of that) wouldn't forget to go. He knew she hadn't forgotten because the night before he saw her looking into their closet with a blank expression. The apartment they had rented from a dentist who wore a toupee and support stockings and asked them for more references and bona fides than they possessed was one room with large windows that looked into a back alley in Kenmore Square. The front of the apartment faced the Charles River and East Cambridge on the other side, but there were no windows to see. The room was a large box with a high ceiling and they had arranged their possessions around the edges of it. Neither was tidy, so these possessions were moving toward the center. Inside the long closet were things hanging that seemed like threads, so skimpy and so hideous. Together, and all crushed together, the simple gaudy dresses and flat skirts looked okay; pushed away from the mates and extras, these items were horrible, bad colors, limp, ugly styles, short skirts that made the knees look like plates; golds and browns, muddy reds and electric blues that turned a sallow face bruise-color. She was thinking this: Kane; and what might he be thinking?—there she is, simple and straight—no, not straight with bunched up shoulders and curling neck, but simple and beautiful—no, not beautiful with cheeks like paste and those hollow eyes, sad and empty; simple and smart—no, not smart when she reads the same sentence over and over trying to squeeze or force it into the tight-packed brain whose retaining walls were close, and impenetrable; simple and sweet— no, she laughed; simple and nothing. I put on my inscrutable form this styleless rag. No, there was a nice, tight pink dress in there, looked like water or leather—no, didn't look like leather, but with laced-up boots—.

"What are you looking for?"

Nothing.

"Don't lie. You're looking for something."

There's a little party at Alex and Jill's. You wouldn't want to go to this, would you?

"No."

It doesn't matter, it'll be—.

She didn't go on. Already, these words had created out of nothing, a heavy and bulky silence. She knew what was in these silences—judgment and accusations. He was weaving a true story of her life at Harvard—all clouded over and mysterious and containing everyone but him; this story was ugly and fabulous; in it, he put all his worries and pains and self-doubts. The story was already enormous. There was so much story, they would need more personal room before long, and where was it going to come from?

She had bounded out of bed, a narrow youth bed they had picked up in a used furniture store, with a metal frame; to push the button of the alarm clock, way across the room underneath the legs of the easel, now closer to the wall with a bright picture of a watercolor bird, red and blue, a good bird, but nearly overflowing the page with a huge wingspread and too small head, no face, seen from the back. She didn't really know where this bird had come from. William Carlos Williams, maybe, whom she loved. He had brought his books with him and this was one of them: Selected Poems. They were nice poems, simple and funny, and in them was an idea of this bird she was sure, although it was probably something else in the poem.

Into the kitchen to put the water on and shovel out measures of coffee into the filter paper. He would wake up when the water hit those beads of coffee, or when the stream started dripping into the glass. "Why," he was already awake, "are you getting yourself up so early to go to this?" She did not, barefoot on the gritty linoleum of the kitchenette, dishes in the sink, and the not quite boiling water in the saucepan, have an answer to this.

This was the way he worked. He questioned. His questions were always good ones and she used them to stop doing the stupid, mindless things she did. With questions like this one, she had left her patients at the mental health center; stopped calling Alex Canfield to chat and go into Cambridge; written a letter to Al and Marie Kane, listing the things they did wrong; threw out a lot of books she wasn't interested in, along with people, ideas, and plans: her Eagle was among the first to go, good riddance. Now she did, on the basis of honest and personal answers to these questions, exactly what she wanted to do, which was nothing: nothing and brooding, nothing and walking, nothing and looking for a job. This tea—Kane had told him it was a party—was the first event since the wedding day in December that she was thinking of going to. "Don't you think this'll be fun?"

He didn't answer this question. He was sitting up in the narrow bed with the sheet around him, smoking a cigarette. In the silence he made, she filled in the things he didn't need to say: he never said what he didn't need to say, so she was getting good at guessing what it might be. She had given him, in the early days, a tale of woes: Alex and Jill, Dr. Marchplace and Nell Beechcroft, Mary Mallon and March Kelly, Martha and every—no, she left out Kasendorf and Jesse, Mark Smith . . . all the boys, because he didn't want to hear about them. He especially didn't want to hear about David Jacobson; he didn't want to hear about any dates or boyfriends—he already hated all these people, but he would listen to stories about the others. He didn't have to listen to many to tell his Anne Marie, whom he loved, how they had hurt, insulted, abused, looked down on, patronized, mocked, undermined, exploited, terrorized, seduced, cadaverized—this was a new one—infantilized, scapegoated, tricked, sucked dry, cremated—she was laughing—eviscerated, macerated—this is stupid, stop—pasteurized, detonated, chewed and spat out like an old dry rind. And good for me, she always added, I deserved it, I even asked for it. You didn't, he said, you didn't know any better, you still don't, like a little dopey baby you are. This changed something. I *am*. And then that changed something. This was being understood and appreciated. A wonderful peacefulness it gave, until she wanted to slip back and sneak back to her old ways, and then it was trouble.

She poured a cup of coffee, milk no sugar, into his cup and sat on a square of sun right on the planks of the floor, no rug. "Why are you down there? Why don't you get in here with me?" There isn't room in there with you. "You don't need that much room, a skinny thing like you." He reached out his hand to pull her onto the little bed, and she spilled some coffee but that was all right; he didn't care about things like that. Her mind was wandering. She couldn't even keep up with it some days; it jigged and jagged. Sometimes he just looked at her, and he could tell what was in there, sometimes not. She would wander like that, up and down, past and present, until something stuck there and she'd go over it and over it until she was done with it, or someone came along and said: hey.

One time, before he did, she had fastened the loose hat of her brain around a simple idea, the same one: the silver platter, and how she had sat on it like a flying saucer and gone spinning down a snowy hill, till it stopped on a patch of snowless grass, all yellow, and stayed there; she got up and rubbed the snow off the snowsuit, wet and spotted with dirt, and it was gone, just the pain from bumping over all those rocks and dry patches, all those jerks and halts, but making it to the bottom with nothing—no big round silver thing—to carry back up. Wait a minute, one more ride, please, on someone else's. I'll take the silver sled of this kid, right here, he isn't even looking. Oh yes he is, give it back. Go back. I'm going. She said this, deciding to walk home, Brookline to Kenmore Square, a pretty day, all light and thin, just a streak of sun now, and no one out yet, even though high tea at high noon in full swing and almost over.

ॐ So he wasn't getting married, so what? So, he wasn't, Miles Kasendorf, LL.D., Harvard University and Phi Beta Kappa, Harvard College, Mensa in high school and gifted before then, going to go back to Paris and marry a French girl, like he said, and start a family now that he was out of law school and free to make the million dollars he needed to live in New York like a pig with his frog, so what? That's what he had said that sad January after the even sadder December when she wasn't supposed to go home but stick around in that freezing house on the fens so she could trot down to the BCMHC and flop flat as a board on the couch and blab in the ear of the stiff sitting in his chair, so handsome and deaf and dumb, while he made a note in his scribble pad and breathed out his pipe smoke so she could see it coming over her head and up higher and out the transom window.

She had talked every morning and brooded every afternoon, eating the weird, contemptible food only a jerk would eat—nothing hot, nothing tasty—and all that time waiting. Waiting for what? For him. He had said: Annie Kane, you are something; and Annie Kane, I want you to enjoy the holiday, you need it; and Annie Kane, I'll only be gone for three weeks; surely, you of all people have something to do during those three weeks; I'd ask you to come with me, but I don't think you can afford it right now, can you? You must be paying a hefty chunk to your shrinker: I've never seen anyone go as much as you do, but I can see the good it's doing you; maybe I should go myself. This late, also he said, the plane tickets would be twice as expensive—did I tell you the deal I got on my ticket? Actually, the deal my father got for me. No? . . . And, Annie Kane, here's what I want you to do while I'm gone. He said: fresh flowers, a string of real pearls, and a steady program of reading; this is what she should get and do. She was the kind of woman who should have a certain life, small and delicate, yet elevated, and much Henry James and Edith Wharton, a little Huysmans and André Gide, essays and letter-writing. And here I am, she thought, with *The M.M.* in hand, covered in snow and intellectual obesity, and not yet finished on the day he arrived and was whisked by taxi to Cambridge, still twenty pages to go.

But she *had*, on one of those freezing afternoons, the sky all cloudy with unfallen snow, taken the subway into Boston and roamed through Filene's Basement to trade in her orange jacket with the fleece lining for a real coat, so elegant and lady-like, camel hair and narrow, with brass buttons and a belt, bought by selling five science textbooks, one borrowed, she had used but never touched with a pencil at good old Christ College and still worth some money, even here, where they mostly didn't use textbooks—none of these professors needed a book to tell them what to do—and with a little Christmas income supposed to be put aside to buy the new books; but she wouldn't need any new books. She wasn't taking any courses you couldn't take the books out of the library for, or borrow them; and writing the thesis, but she didn't know what books she'd need for that; the typing paper she could get at home. She put this coat on with its soft surface when she got the call and was to meet, at the end of the endless vacation when she had moved to the dorm because the house was so gloomy and cold and scary at night, then back to the house because the dorm was so empty and quiet and scary at night, and finally back to the dorm, Miles Kasendorf, at a little restaurant on Mass. Avenue called the Midget, a deli with all its sandwiches and plates named after Radcliffe.

There he was at the counter with his spoon in a cup of black coffee and the black coat and new scarf—a white scarf with a fringe—so handsome and so fat. Was he fat? She couldn't remember if he was fat like now, or whether he just looked fat. Let me look at you, he said, after kissing her cheek and pinching her arm with a big white hand; she could see he was holding her as far away from him as he could: when she tried to move forward to give him back a kiss, she couldn't—his arm was stiff and she was at the end of it. This was the first sign that something wasn't right.

She wanted to tell him she had done everything he said: a bunch of dried blue flowers was on her bureau in a little vase she found at home that Ellen and she had used for their May altars and the grandmother had a strand of pink pearls she didn't need that Annie Kane was wearing over a black cardigan sweater, no blouse, just a sweater and just the pearls: it must have been impressive because even the girls at dinner stared and Martha had said: where are you off to, madam, looking so slinky? But she didn't get a chance to take off the new coat and show him; she didn't get a chance to draw his attention to the new coat that wasn't orange and puffy but sleek and light brown: he didn't seem to notice. He said: let's sit somewhere; I've got some great news to tell you, and he said he was marrying his Paris girlfriend whom he had just gone over to see and spend Christmas vacation with. Her parents had agreed and back he would go this summer, immediately after Harvard graduation, with his parents the doctors who would fly over with him if his father could get away from the practice, which he was sure he could do: he had said, and Miles quoted him, what's more important than the marriage of my son? Only one thing, the marriage of my son to a beautiful French princess, also a lawyer, and in Paris in the springtime, that's what. Miles was sounding excited, but his face was grim-looking and his eyelid was twitching. His pink cheeks were very pink and he had reached his hand over to hold Annie Kane's arm.

Annie Kane, Radcliffe junior and analysand, removed the arm from the table. No. She *thought* she removed the arm from the table, but looking down, it was still there with the hand wrapped around it, and now he was noticing her coat and paying it many compliments. When he finished and had drunk the rest of his coffee and told the waiter no, he didn't want any more, but maybe the lady would like to order; but the lady said no, there was a brief silence and no one else in the restaurant on a Monday night before the first day of classes was there to fill that silence: even the waiter and sandwich man were silent. Miles looked at his watch. It was a new watch. Was it a new watch or a new watchband? He said it was a leather watchband from Italy his prospective father-in-law, M. Guy, had given him. Who? Alain Guy, Madeleine's father—he owns a chain of drugstores. After another minute of silence, during which a student came in, jingled the bells over the door and ordered a corned beef on rye, country fries and a large coke, Anne Kane found something to talk about: she knew she wanted to say something and finally here it was: I'm reading, she said to Miles Kasendorf, whose face suddenly relaxed and you could see the depression underneath the glee—she had seen this before—Mann's *Magic Mountain*. "Really? That's wonderful." I'm reading, she said; I've *been* reading for three weeks now. It's taking me a very long time. "That's not long," he said, "it took me a year. I still haven't finished it." I'm going to finish it, she said, I'm almost finished. "I knew you'd like Mann," he said.

I hate it, she said, I hate this book. Now Miles's face was even more relaxed; it was slack and all deflated. "You do?" It's the stupidest book I've ever read in my life and the most hateful. "Surely," he said, "you're exaggerating." It's sentimental, she said. It's full of hysteria. I haven't believed anything that's happened so far, any single feeling or any single conversation. It's, she said, looking at that face so like a pudding, totally—remembering this now, crossing the street on this bright morning, she had to smile: she loved the book—it was the story of her life the way this life should have been; every smart thing said in the book she believed: it was all true, Settembrini and Naphta, they were both right; Hans Castorp was a little nit, sure, but the life he had up there was the perfect life and now she knew exactly what this life would be if you could have it—fraudulent.

This conversation, if you could call it that, was fast brought to a close. "It's not the book you despise," Miles said after Annie K. had attacked the book for five minutes, "it's me and you know it." Do you think, she said and this was what pushed him out the door and down the street with no goodbye, although she saw him again the next day, your life, *your* personality are the equal of that big novel? He didn't, Miles didn't know what to say to this and besides, Annie Kane, slow reader, didn't know what she meant by it: she wasn't even sure whether it was an insult or a way to make him feel better, off the hook. Was he, as he walked out insulted and defamed, by being smaller than *The Magic Mountain* on the hook, she wondered, or off it? She looked up: there was the waiter with the check for the coffee.

☙ Too much coffee was what she was thinking, unlocking the apartment door, and now I have to spend the rest of the day feeling rotten. Opening the door, there was Mr. Frazier sitting on the bed with his guitar; and a little glass of something and looking at the bird, which he had taken off the easel and pinned to the wall. It was the only thing on the wall.

The next day, a Monday, she trod across Massachusetts Avenue because she had seen a sign on the New England Deli: Help Wanted. Inside was a little restaurant, very hot, with a counter piled high with things to eat, oversized cookies and large pickles, long and wide loaves of bread, huge brownies and a mountain of white and brown candy like sand all pounded together: Halvah, they called it; it was very sweet and crumbly, made, they said, from sesame but there were no seeds that she could see. This candy was under a cellophane tent, but you could touch it on the sides. They carved pieces of it and wrapped it up in paper. She didn't know when you were supposed to eat this candy, and whether it went with something else, like brown sugar on grapefruit; no, it didn't go on grapefruit. Seeing this mound while she was filling out an employment questionnaire with a small pencil and sitting up there at the counter, she stopped the pencil and laid it down on its back. There had been two mountains of this candy at a party she had gone to last year, senior year. Spring, because they were outside without coats, and inside was an all pastel house, pink chairs and blue chairs, pale couches and pale rugs, and the queen of this party was the girl cousin of David Jacobson, all in pastel, thin and smiling.

It was an all-Jewish party but Anne Kane didn't feel awkward; it was just a family party with talk and eating. The girl queen was going to work for the summer at a big hospital with her dad, a surgeon. She had always wanted to be a doctor, David Jacobson had already told A.M. Kane, Cliffie, even though, he said in his usual way, she's not a Radcliffe girl like you. Like me. Like I am? Like you so much want to be. This girl, Amy or Emily, wanted to be a doctor so bad, she entered medical school in her junior year of college. She stopped college, the most fun you ever have in your life, according to some people, and went off to medical school, nineteen years old, skirts and sweaters, boots and flats, blouses and party dresses, like the one she had on: pink and silky, and long slender legs. A girl with glasses, A.M. recognized the type: a pretty dress and glasses, no makeup. This type was everywhere and you could always trust it: a kind of Martha, but maybe not as interesting as Martha.

Martha was not around to be interesting: she was in England, one semester, writing the history of the bathtub, and with a grant because what an interesting idea it was, so unlike the ordinary senior thesis, blah blah blah, history, theory, and application, respectfully submitted in partial fulfillment. A.M.K. had planned to write one too, but not as interesting, more goofy than interesting. But this one, early medical, didn't even get to the point of writing one, David Jacobson had said many times. She did nothing but science, and after completing all the courses in one year and a half, her father arranged for her to take the medical boards and her scores were stratospheric, he said. She liked his words. Off the girl went to her father's medical school, Albert Einstein. It was spring, a spring party for a girl on a little vacation, and back home in New York state, and she had the time to come to a party like this, relax and talk to friends, like her best friend and cousin, David Jacobson, and her second best friend, David Jacobson's girlfriend.

Emily had already visited Jacobson and girlfriend at Harvard. He had said how he had always had a little crush on this younger cousin, so studious and so intense, and A.M. thought he might still have it. Holding hands, she saw it, while the three of them were lying on the floor, Kirkland House L-43, listening to the Velvet Underground. He did that, though; that was like him. Emily Goldstein stayed two days and had many intense talks with her older cousin, who tried to convince her to drop out of med school and spend a year at Harvard as a special student, doing nothing, seeing the world, easing up. He kept them up all one night whispering and talking, making tea and filling the hash pipe, playing record after record, talking and talking, until Emily said she would: she'd call her father in the morning and tell him, and they all went to bed on that idea. David had rolled the twin bed into the bedroom and they all slept in one room to hold onto this resolve, but by morning, it was gone. She was pale and a little sick, Emily Goldstein, and already anxious, A.M. could see it, because she had missed a day of classes and was overtired. David wanted to take her alone to the plane and he did, right after breakfast. They all trudged, tired and headachey, into the Square for a sickening breakfast at the Hayes-Bickford, David's favorite restaurant because it was open all night and filled with hideous characters, and even more hideous cooks and servers.

Emily ate a rim of one half of an English muffin and a teaspoonful of tomato juice, one sip of weak tea, and excused herself. David Jacobson called a cab and whisked her to the airport. She said, giving A.M. a hug and a kiss, that she was just starting to feel better, but A.M. knew it was because she was going; she would be on the plane in a half hour and all by herself, and could open her biochemistry book, a thick book of formulas and molecules, and study pages and pages with her photographic memory, certain she was on the right path, gratified, as A.M. could see she was, that David Jacobson, an artist and a genius, had given her a chance to freak out, to be young. She had had it and it was over. A.M. Kane, who trudged back to L-43 to brood and eat butterscotch candies, the only thing in the house, thought this girl Emily Goldstein was about as lucky as you could get. She knew what she was doing, even though what she was doing was hard and boring. Maybe it wasn't boring, A.M. whispered in a voice: how do *you* know what's boring and what isn't. She had climbed back into the bed and let her tired eyes rest on the pile of clothes, books, and dirt in the horrible room. So unlike, she was thinking, any room that girl would live in then or now. And where would she be by now? Anne Kane had picked up the pencil again; the application was asking about previous experience, dates and places: "Haverhill Community . . . " Emily Goldstein, at the end of her first year in medical school, and because of the surprise decision by the Einstein faculty (the "Einstein faculty"—this was a wonderful thing: bristly old doctors with curled-up fingers, who knew everything and inquired into everything), was accelerated and allowed to do med school in three years flat, as David Jacobson had told Anne Kane, full of pride; she'd be, he said, in a surgical residency, probably in her father's hospital by 1978, think of that.

She was thinking about it. Dr. Goldstein was almost there. She was moving fast, and other people just as fast. And where was Anne Marie Kane going (Education: A.B., Radcliffe College; Work Experience: Art Workshop, HCMHC)? and how fast? Backwards, still going backwards. Slowly, very slowly, as if any of the things that had ever happened really mattered, when what did she amount to for all of that? Nothing. She was something a little like a mule she had seen in a black-and-white movie: the mule just stood; it was wounded; it stood there under the hot sun while the flies collected on its sides and started to eat it. Someone tried to get the mule to move, but it wouldn't. It stood there in the sun and was eaten in from the sides.

The man said, thanks: "we'll call you; we need someone, but we wanted someone with experience. You don't have any, do you? Well, we might call you anyway. We need someone right away. Can you come right away? If you can come right away, you've got a job. When can you come? Come on Wednesday four o'clock, and someone'll be here to show you. You don't have a white uniform? Get yourself a little white dress; you can get those dresses anywhere and we'll give you the apron. Put your hair in that ponytail; that's right. Good. Be here at four, nice to meet you, ah Anne, it's Anne, isn't it? Is it Annie or Anne? Anna? Oh, Anna. It says Anne here. Oh, I guess it doesn't.

Your handwriting isn't so good. Anna, I see. Anna, see you Wednesday, four sharp, in a uniform.

Anna, large with a spindly ponytail, issued from the hot deli to the wide square and attempted to cross the street in front of a car, little car, tiny Honda, slammed on its brakes. Hey. She ran across the rest of the street, didn't look back. It was nice to be out, free, in the sunshine and all of a sudden there she was, on March 25, in front of the subway entrance, standing there, and the subway calling her: yoohoo. Down she sent, down the hole. Two blocks and she would have been home safe, but no; down the hole. See you. She was (get out of here) going (forget it) to run (says who?) away.

FOUR THINGS

These are the four things to consider: misery, Catholics, interlude, fig, and how they relate and share a being. Misery, as I've
heard say, is always the first to arrive and brings with it its own
cape of sentiment, a swing beat, and the fumes of a misery headache. You can sometimes see it coming, breathing through its nose,
and angling like that for a kiss. Give it a blow; no one gives it
a blow and lets it taste its own blood, and its blood is filth, just
as you thought, you others.

Once it has arrived, and first in place, guide its little hand along
the wall and let it feel the accumulation there from its other visits:
the threads and noodles, the scratch and grooves, the mixture
of things and wet plaster in that one place. Here is misery, tell
your friends, here is who he is, smile into his face; see how bright
he is, and all mouth.

The Catholics are nearly all men and deep within their gloom,
the gloom of a life in space, of the space in the mind, of the cracks
and jellies in the cracks, of the singular thinness of Jesus' body
in a misery wafer. This is their life and at least some part of it
could be yours. Come, men, fill out your cheeks with the filling
breath, the wonderful wind of faith. Come, men, fill out those
bulging eyes and let them fill with the lovely spectacle of continu-
ing good works, the memory of all the saints—all the splits and
holes in consciousness, a new worm for it, just you wait.

Aurora dawn, the incessant but broken flow of beatitudes
creates the boundary between night and day, when all the Catholics line behind their doors and misery in the trees sends up its
sweet babble, a chain of toys and everything that fell to earth, fell
back to earth, that is, or was, was not manna but some of these
trinkets, too, misery cords and misery strings. But here, at that
moment, the welt of day, a striking blow or interlude or space for
silence and just waiting, a sort of nest-building or speculation,
if you can ignore those tree-hanging miseries and the heavy, lowing Catholics bumped up against the door.

Finally, interlude, played or dropped to its full and singing a
thin, and then pleasant kind of nothingness, the fourth thing, and
all good things come in one of those picnic baskets, and we're

already here waiting for it. A fig is spread, its seeded flesh and particular odor, in this tough, fanned bag with a knot tied as tough and miserable as a Catholic with a lump of faith and ashes to ashes could close a death sack, a mighty twist, and pouf, the night of sins disappears behind its sentimental curtain and trees grow up a million of misery birds. This fig, take it, eat, it's a fig or finger from the head of God and his multiplicity, take it while he is hanging his laundry out, and these blackbirds circling around his bald and pitted head.

O misery, o darkling, a breed of Catholics in their winter gloom and pressed for certainty, the interlude of the earth's own pleasant pastime and a fig for the ferment, and outside this house the transparent dream of the laughing clothes.

NNE Kane was in the new room, January 20, with the new roommate; the new roommate, Rickee Glasheen, had gone home for the weekend, a nice girl; her father had picked her up in the family car, very ordinary, and driven her home; they asked a million times, both of them, if Annie (or Roomie, as Rickee called Annie) would go with, but Annie—who liked Rickee and whose relief at having this pleasant, frenzied girl from Quincy as a partner, who played the guitar, practiced karate, sang in the Russian choir, was very giddy, loved her roomie, and was always giving her a hug and making her do something for the fun of it, and with a full set of friends, which opened like the Red Sea to admit the fleeing Is, was great; what could be better? Nothing, except once in a while, the roomie liked staying in the room all by herself and enjoying the peaceful hours—said no, and gave Rickee a hug in return and a promise to be home in the room on Sunday night when Rickee Glasheen's boyfriend, Zoro, would drive her back and then they could meet. Roomie had already seen Zoro, when he and Rickee worked on the back steps of the dorm, cracking wood blocks with their feet and hands; Zoro, B.C., geography, was an expert. He always wore a red bowtie, just 5'5"; he and Rickee seemed more like brother and sister to Roomie, and Rickee had a million complaints and tears about him. Behind his back, she had taken to calling him Pip, so now Roomie called him that: Pip. His real name Roomie didn't know; Rickee never used his real name. Even Mr. Glasheen called him Zoro, but it was, Rickee had explained early on and then to every new person, not for Zorro who makes the sign of the Z, it was for Zoroaster and a certain expertise that Zoro, or Pip, had with Tarot cards.

These cards had first come into the picture in freshman English, when the teacher, Dr. McEnerney, had told them to buy "The Wasteland" by T. S. Eliot, and a few of the cards were in that poem. Some of the songs that were popular: Bob Dylan, The Jefferson Airplane, mentioned these cards, too, and Anne Marie was anxious to see what they looked like; they didn't sound like ordinary playing cards at all, and they weren't. Anne Marie found a deck in Cambridge, pretty: each cards had a figure, some repeats, but the figures, very interesting and not clear in their meaning, unless you knew a lot about them. Anne Marie was on a day trip to Boston with her new friend, Sooky, a girl who drove her father's lavender Cadillac and had a new fox fur that season. Sooky liked Anne Marie because they were in the same French class (See, you didn't think you'd make friends besides that hateful, her mother had said, Kelly Girl, but you did. I told you you would and you did.) and were smart. It was Sooky's best and only subject: she hated college, hated Christ College, hated all the subjects, hated studying, and went home every weekend, right after the Saturday morning class that everyone had to go to, but didn't come back for Sunday morning chapel, which everyone had to go to or face the dean of students, Sister John Mary, on Monday morning for what they called a conference, but was really a lot of inquisitive remarks and a sermon.

Anne Marie had been there, but for other reasons.

Sooky gathered up her things from her neat blue room—like a lady chapel, perfect and quiet—and packed them in two white leather suitcases, and then the fox coat. She left these suitcases, all packed, near the door and spent Friday night sitting in bed—Anne Marie had seen her and tried to cheer her up—talking to her mother on her private phone and crying. Other people went to mixers or into Boston; Sooky, so pretty and such wonderful clothes, all strange; nothing Anne Marie had ever seen before; stayed in the dorm. Anne Marie didn't understand this.

One time Sooky asked Anne Marie to come into Boston on a Saturday: first meet around twelve o'clock, Copley Square, and they could shop, eat lunch, shop, eat dinner, go to a movie, and meet their French teacher, Mlle Marie Goff, in her apartment in Cambridge for tea. Mlle Goff had invited them a few times and Anne Marie was dying to do it, but didn't know how to go about it. Sooky did. You get into Boston, you call Mlle Goff on the phone—her number's in the book, I've seen it—and, if it works out and she's free, you drop by after a show just for a little while, no big deal. Mlle Goff was a young teacher with pale blonde hair and a tired face; she was full of ideas about French writers and full of gloom and pessimism about life, which was very exciting to hear. She came into the classroom— Sooky and Anne Marie sitting side by side in the middle of the room, way down in the basement of College Hall—always in a different tailored suit. She was thin with a high, squeaky voice and sometimes a deep squeaky voice, depending on what her subject was: French writers or life. She always looked sad, with big circles under her eyes and long skinny fingers pressed on the desk, bending under the weight of her whole body. She spoke a beautiful French, much more realistic sounding than the nuns, and had told Sooky and Anne Marie, her pets, to go straight to France on a Fulbright, to major in

French and go on to graduate school. Anne Marie wasn't sure, but Sooky was already signed up and prepared to drop all her other courses, if only she could.

None of the girls in her old corridor was in this French class because it was advanced and they were in beginning everything, so Anne Marie felt safe from their glances and remarks. She had gone, that one Saturday, to Sister John Mary when she didn't think she could stand it anymore: how they ignored her and laughed behind her back. What am I doing that's bothering you so much? she had begged March Kelly late one night. Kelly, as March now wanted to be called, had returned to the bedroom as late as she possibly could—lights out was at 11:15—and jumped into bed, faced the wall. I don't know what you're talking about, she said, but first waited a few minutes to see if she had to answer at all. March, are you awake? the roommate said. March Kelly had told Barbara and Jo that she didn't even like to say the girl's name. Yes, she said, in a voice that sounded like it was coming deep out of the ground.

Did you hear me?

I heard you; how could I not hear you; you're right there.

Well?

You're not doing anything; you study all the time; you don't have time for anything.

Anne Marie heard this in the dark of the room and thought Kelly sounded funny; this was not her voice.

Is that why you all hate me?

Is what why? Kelly said.

It was a friendly voice; how could that be? Anne Marie had heard this voice when March Kelly was talking to Barbara and Jo, Carol and Isabel, Jane and Phoebe.

Is that why you don't like me, that I study all the time? I *don't* study all the time. I hardly study at all.

Yes you do, Kelly said in an exhausted tone. We always see you in the library.

You do?

What do *you* think?

Anne Marie stopped to think what this meant. The shades were up; no one had closed them, and she could see the black sky, but not that well, because no glasses. It might not even be a black sky; it could be clouded for all she knew. March?

What?

All along you've—and everybody else—had nothing against me?

91

What could we have against you? You're perfectly nice, plus you're so quiet, who even knows you're here. You never talk to *me*.

Yes I do.

I hadn't noticed.

A rush of speech came to the tired mouth of Anne Marie and she let some of it out, but not all; it was late and she wasn't sure March Kelly meant any of the things she said; but some of it came out, and the girl heard. She was being nice in return and said just as much, and pretty soon the atmosphere in the hateful room was friendly and they both fell asleep, Anne Marie full of the mystery of this: how could it be? How could this go on for so long: it was November, right before Thanksgiving, and be so hard and yet be nothing; or something you could clear up in one night?

When Anne Marie woke up—late—the next morning, March Kelly was already gone, dressed and gone, and everything neat on her side: something new. "Wait and see, that's the best policy," her mother said on the phone because every Sunday they talked at 11:30, right after chapel. March had been in chapel. Anne Marie saw her up in front where she always sat with the two girls next door and the rest of the corridor in the row before and the row after. "You've forgotten already," her mother went on, "the rotten things she's done to you. Are you going to forget all that just on her say-so? I don't believe that girl's changed in one night, no matter what you say.

"She doesn't like you, I could see that from the first day. If I could see it, why can't you?—you're smart."

Her mother, Mrs. Kane, forty-eight years old, high school graduate, full-time secretary, housewife and mother—she went back to work as soon as Anne Marie went to college: "If you can do it, I can do it," she said over the phone, "so I did it," and now Mrs. Kane could get out of the house and away from screaming children and yelling husband and bellyaching mother every single day and no one could say otherwise; it, the job at the valve company, was a complete success and they talked about it every Sunday during the phone call: I'm doing, the mother said, almost as good as you're doing and you never hear me complaining; I love it, I love getting out among people—was right. Anne Marie Kane, 18½ years old, three months into college, all girls', honor roll student, math and physics major, and a real student ("She's," her mother would tell people, "a real student, you know, not like the rest of them including that crummy roommate, thinks she's so great because the father works downtown, so what? I work downtown, tell her that.") was wrong; March Kelly, conversation or no, didn't change one whit. She hated and despised, ignored and mocked her roommate just as much. Then why had she said what she said that one night? That one night they talked so nice to each other? This question, even Mrs. Kane wanted to know, and asked her husband Al, who said: How should I know, Marie, I didn't even hear the story.

This kind of aimless question made him mad, so Mrs. Kane asked Anne Marie—you could ask Anne Marie anything—instead. "Why: do you know why?" Anne Marie started a big long song-and-dance on the phone, of theories and ideas, but Mrs. Kane—this wasn't what she wanted at all—couldn't bear it, the tedium of it, and shut the girl off. "Listen, you don't know any more than the man in the moon. Face it, you just don't get along. She doesn't want to be friends, can't you get that through your head? Why don't you go out and find that pretty girl, you know, Doreeto, she likes you, she'll be your friend."

Anne Marie waited another month, then right before Christmas went to the dean of students and put up with the inquiries and the sermon, but got what she wanted in the end, a switch, and a switch over to some girls Anne Marie knew just a little; they didn't hate her—she knew that much—and the nun, after talking to her *and* March Kelly, and then talking to her again and saying how March Kelly didn't really want her to go, it was all her own doing, her imagination, the nun was ready to say, but held it back because these girls weren't children after all, let her do what she wanted. She couldn't believe she was doing it the day she did it—March Kelly must have known the day, because the whole corridor was empty of girls; they had all gone off somewhere because one of them now had a car, and Anne Marie slowly moved her things one by one, two by two, down the hall. After a while, the new girls saw what she was doing and how pathetic it was: thing by thing, and some of them helped her and asked her to go to dinner with them and it was all going to work out, she told her mother that next day, she knew it would. Keep your fingers crossed, the mother said.

But it *did* work out; Anne Marie Kane had friends coming out of her ears, as her mother said, and happy as can be. They're not, Marie said to Al, as down on her as they used to be for studying all the time; she can study as much as she wants for all they care; that's what she told me. Some of *them* study too. Isn't that what they're there for?

Why is that so surprising? She asked Anne Marie, but Anne Marie didn't have the answer.

In her own mind (why don't they study?), Anne Marie pictured bridge table, cigarette machine, coffee shop, dungaree skirts, phonograph records, Sam and Dave, the Rolling Stones, going to Boston, signing out for the weekend, horse shows (this was a new one and not everybody did it). She was herself, on a day when she should be reading the Old Testament—it took a long time to get the week's book read, plus the other books from the other classes and sometimes the recommended reading—going into Boston on an expedition which would take up day and night and even a little bit of Sunday getting over it and thinking about it.

Thinking about it in the hot dorm room, still and dark, gloomy and dark, with a heavy smell of sleep, although there was only the one sleeping in it, looking out to see how, late in the night, snow had fallen, and the ground and cars were covered with a thick pad, buildings and trees; no sound, just a whistle as the wind stirred the loose snow; dropping the shade and sitting on the warm bed, she regretted it. It was late, 12:30 Sunday afternoon, and there was not enough time to read, study, do the math problems, wash clothes, eat dinner and spend Sunday night the way these girls—Roomie would be back—liked to spend Sunday night, together in someone's room, talking about boys and then driving out to Bailey's in Wellesley for a sundae. Last night—she couldn't even say the words, too exciting—had to be forgotten. She tried to push it down, all the thoughts and impressions, by rushing into the bathroom—quiet, everyone was at lunch—and steaming it out of her in the shower.

Who, since you're so smart and have time to gallivant day and night, restaurants and bars and movie theaters and cold white wine, heresies and subjects you know nothing about, are the various anonymous narrators, P, D, JE, and H, of the five books of Genesis, and what is implied by the different stylistic strands and their origins? You don't know, do you? You're not that sure—you can't distinguish them that well. You're just too full of bullshit to notice, or to take the time to notice. Tell me! What were you doing, Good Friday afternoon, while Jesus was hanging on the cross for your sins? Your lips were flapping, your eyes were open and gaping. How do you explain a girl, nineteen years old, sleeping till 12:30, Miss Kane, neglect her studies, hurt the little baby Jesus with pins and prods of negligence and misery, the fifteen or forty-five deadly venial sins, although this one was mortal, bone lazy.

Get down on your knees and thank your patron saint, St. Maria Beelzebub, Rose of Lima, Maria Doreeta Goretti, Martin Luther, the Little Flame, Gregory the Great, Lazarus, Tiger Lily, Martin and Catherine of Siena, James the Lesser, John Chrysostom, the Blessed Mary Madeleine Victoire, and the Ace of Spades, that Jesus and his angels don't strike you dead in the night with your arm sticking up out of the grave for that time you tried to strike your mother, you hateful girl. This was good and the shower was burning her fat and tough back, thick-skinned and perverse, turning away from all that was good and holy, worthwhile and wholesome, turning toward that ugly, sinful face, lecherous, gluttonous, slothful, faithless, tempted, grievous, proud, slanderous, and full of envy for everything that is sickening and sinful, corrupt and deadly in the world. O world, legs and arms, enter my soul and sting it; all my greedy mouths are open, fill me with your stench.

This was today's prayer and she covered the flesh, all pink and burnt, fingertips wrinkled by water, eyes red and stung, lips chapped, shivering now because the hot water had long run out, with a thin flannel bathrobe, taken from home, one of Jimmy's from when he was a boy, and she was thinner now, thin and snake-like, long skinny legs: trouble.

It was a nice dull day full of hot rooms, hangover, sick stomach and reading in bed all by herself, cut off from the world, a paradise. One book followed another and the bed was strewn with paperbacks and hardbacks, sheets of loose-leaf paper, an apple core, Kleenex and Tums' wrappers. She had pulled the shade down and turned all the lights on. Sunday was a quiet day anyway: boys and parents came to take the students on an outing. A message would come over the loudspeaker: Cathy Haven, you have a visitor, and someone would fling open a door and start tearing up and down the corridor, with girls tearing after her, metal rollers, makeup mirror, bathrobe and slippers, ribbon, iron, stockings, powdery perfume, and then suddenly it would be quiet again until: "Mary Beth Akins, you have a caller," or "Jane Phillipides, call on the second floor." Door flung open and loud feet on the linoleum floor. This happened all afternoon. Miss Kane could picture the cars streaming into Boston and streaming out to Wellesley, or up to Worcester, or just a pretty girl in a blue or tan suit sitting in the formal parlor with a date, B.C., Holy Cross, or going on the grounds to smoke a cigarette or drink from a flask: sloe gin fizz, rum coke, 7 and 7, brandy alexander, screwdriver, B and B, highball, whiskey sour, scotch old-fashioned, tequila sunrise, planter's punch, margarita, coke float, lime freeze. She was already, in her mind, across the street and into the meadow where the reservoir was, so might as well go as sit here with dead eyes on a dead page, when "Anne Marie Kane, you have a visitor," came over the loudspeaker.

One foot was on the cold floor, the other asleep on the bed and tingling. She could see herself from there, and in that funny position, in the mirror, goofy, hideous—hair going the wrong way, face like a white button, and all covered over with a facial masque she had left on for an hour, thinking it would do extra good to let it freeze there until it cracked on its own. The only thing moving were the eyelids and the awful hair, wild as an animal. If only the foot would wake up and stop sleeping. She beat it on the floor, then on Rickee's woven rug, but still it felt all crinkled and electric. And someone was pounding on the door.

"Anne Marie Kane?"

Just a minute.

"You have a call."

She limped to the door, ran to the phone and dialed the desk, but the line was busy. She dialed again, breathing hard, and still busy. Then, it was ringing, but no one was answering. She dialed again, embarrassed at the thought of the yellow phone down there in the receiving booth, the little alcove where the housemother sat—Miss Mattson, gray hair and neat tweed suit, tie shoes with a thick slab of rubber sole—she probably got up to go to the bathroom, or wasn't down there at all: some student maybe was doing the bells duty and had run off to get a Coke in the laundry room, or to the library to return a reserve book, or to talk to somebody in a parked car. "Yes?" What? "This is the desk." Oh, thank you. "Can I help you?" I . . . "Anne Kane?" Yes? "You have a caller," and then the bells person hung up. Miss Kane, face red and burning, sweaty and tense under the plaster cast now starting to crumble, and little pieces of it on the phone receiver, dialed again. "Yes?" Can you tell me who it is, please? "Who is this?" Anne Kane. Can you tell me who the caller is? I'm sorry to bother you, but—. "Wait a minute. I'll ask him."

Even before the girl, who had dropped the receiver hard on the desk, returned to pick it up again, Miss Kane knew, from the sound of her voice (she knew who this girl was, Bettina Thomas, pretty with long black hair and a perfect, hard face, a junior pinned to a boy at Harvard: every Saturday in the fall, she dressed in a bright, solid-color suit with a velvet cape and high black boots, and went with the Harvard boy to a Harvard football game in Cambridge. She was beautiful and would be married, everybody knew this, on graduation day or shortly after, and was now in the process of working a little, a few hours a week, to help her parents—father a tailor, mother a housewife, but everything they had or would ever have, went to the thing they loved most, Bettina; they drove up every Sunday afternoon from Chelmsford to see her and bring her a present of fruit or cake, or a new blouse or skirt; Bettina left the cake or fruit in the smoker, and went to one meal a day, dinner, to keep herself thin as a blade—pay for a wedding in Boston at a hotel in Copley Square. The girl had never spoken to Anne Marie Kane, but there was something in her voice now that was friendly) that the girl was impressed. "He says his name is Michael Fury. He looks familiar. Do I know him? Where did you meet him?" Anne Marie, whose feet were freezing and face stinging from the sweat and the masque, was starting to say—when Bettina said: "Listen, you better hurry. This guy's already been waiting down here ten minutes."

She met him—the masqued girl thought, if it was who she thought it was, as she was steaming herself again to get the white hard paste to unstick, and then powdering her damp skin and dumped the powder all over the tile floor, drying her hair in clumps with Roomie's hair blaster, the most powerful hairdryer on earth so it only took a few minutes, but the hairs, each one, were quivering with static and arranging themselves like a cloud of wires around her ears, pulled on a red sweater, very soft, over this galvanic mass and it thrilled and chattered once more in the air; a black skirt, nylons and gray shoes with stacked heels, nice shoes, bought on sale yesterday in Filene's Basement, an hour or so before—on the subway going to Cambridge to give the French teacher a call in her apartment, which they never got to. They ended up, Sooky and Ooky, which is what one of the boys who picked them up decided, hearing one name, what the twin names must be, so cute and so alike they were, typical townies from . . . where? Where were they from? some Catholic college, women's college in the suburbs, and you know how Catholic and sex are two words for the same thing, meeting Ted and Ed, which is what Ooky called *them*, smartaleck, both a little tipsy, hanging onto the railing on the red line to Harvard Square and doing funny things, saying funny things, exactly alike, two Harvard boys with penny loafers and Harris tweeds. I know who you are, Oolong—they changed it to Oolong when they heard the tongue that came out and the tone that came with it—had said.

"Hi, may I introduce my friend?" Ted had said, glittery eyes popped and stuck in the middle of a beautiful boy's face, all sleek and horsey with a hard, pointy chin. The thick, smooth skin of Sooky's neck and cheeks was streaked with red and the red was climbing up to her eyes. She was suddenly so red, Anne Marie thought she might blow up. "Don't interrupt," Anne Marie turned to the twins, then finished saying what she had been saying about the old days and the tricks the awful March had played on her, but she could tell Sooky wasn't listening, so Oolong turned around to the Harvard team, hovering, and all pink in their faces, too, and said: "Didn't your mothers teach you any manners? This is a private conversation," but said it in such a way and with a grin that the two stringy boys, dangling off the pole they had attached themselves too, and on their way back from a mixer at—guess where? Christ College, and on a dare from their suitemates ("What a couple of snobs you are," the new Oolong said, hearing this a few minutes later) to go out and meet Catholics, loved it. Ted said to Ed: "Well, we'll wait then, till they're finished," then turned back to Oolong with his head resting on his hand, midair, and a polite expression. Now Sooky's face was white and her mouth white.

This is how they got started. And how they ended up was hot dogs at the Hayes-Bickford, big beers at the Plough and Stars, coffee in the Pewter Pot and three-legged races across the Harvard Yard to where these two boys lived, Kenilworth: they were freshmen, stupid and giddy as girls, Oolong thought. They played and they drank and ate till it was time to get back on the subway and into Boston, so Sooky could drive Oolong, the drunken boat, back to campus in the lavender Cadillac, but no: instead, Sooky's father, when he saw O and S and heard them laughing, drove the girls back to college, after making them some black coffee and throwing in—their father was a good egg—some brandy because he was enjoying them, his own girl so rarely had a smile on her serious face.

How much, though, Anne Marie thought, standing all dressed and perfect, rammed and jammed, curled and painted, oiled and powdered, and so stiff she couldn't move her mouth if she wanted to—the room still shaded from the sun, every light blazing—had she done that was wrong, when she couldn't even remember what she had done? They played, they laughed, they rolled on the hard, freezing ground of the Harvard yard, then they warmed up at the Hayes-Bickford, ran down to the river and chased each other across the bridge and onto the other side. It was night and you're not, a girl, supposed to be out at night drinking with boys you don't even know: so, there was that, then missing Mass on Sunday and Holy Days of Obligation, bad thoughts (dirty thoughts?) and that kind of thrill and excitement, chasing and rolling, that's outlawed from any perspective. Guilty, she said to the mirror, then showed the thousand teeth tablets in a smile. Go then, if you're going to go, go. She flew and hammered down the dormitory steps, happy heels, and hideous full smiles.

They did other things, too. What? Ooky didn't want to say, even to herself, but she remembered some roughhouse, hugs and grips, pushes and rolls—it all seemed okay on the surface, but was it?

It was the same boy, Michael J. ("What's the J stand for?") Fury ("Jayzus"); he was dressed in the skins of old dungarees and dungaree coat, a fresh white shirt, with a face as pure and sweet as a baby's.

"How do you do," he said sticking his hand out to this primped and taut element, all the traces of laziness chipped and soaked out, just a springy blade, a wire, a Scout. "It is you, isn't it? Oolong? Or is it," he paused and whispered, " . . . Anne Marie Kane?"

It's me.

The boy was looking around the room, all tedious and velvet, a high sheen on all the wood and the old red Turkey carpet on the floor, enough to make you cry. "Is this where you live?"

This is where I live; this is where you live when you're a freshman. The nuns, she said, pointing to a tunnel in the wall, a glassed-in passage-way with chintz curtains and dark sofas, live down there. We're connected day and night. They race in and out, inspection every hour, holy things are always going on, so be careful.

He turned his head to Oolong so she could get the benefit of his thick, bright hair and laughing face, the cutest boy she'd ever seen in her life; but she turned her eyes so he couldn't see her seeing this.

"Oolong?"

What?

"Can we get out of here or are you chained? Where's your chain? I'll bite it off with these," he said, pointing to his big cute mouth, Pepsodent teeth, not all riddled with holes and fillings, not huge brilliant tablets sticking straight out at an eager angle, no: just perfect. "Beautiful teeth you have," she said; "are they your own?"

"What?"

"Nothing."

They tramped out into the day and onto the path cleared of snow.

"It's pretty out here, you know?"

"No, it isn't."

"It is, in a way, but what do you do all day long?"

Oolong had a smart answer sliding over the ends of the buck teeth, but stopped it. "I study. We take five courses, you know, and a few of them meet on Saturday, 9 A.M."

"I don't believe it."

They were walking in the parking lot toward a little red car. Oolong didn't know the popular names of cars, so it could be any car, small and shiny, two seats instead of four. "It's true. Is that yours?"

"No, it's my roommate's. I don't have a car, do you? No, you don't have a car; I can tell that."

"How do you know I don't have a car. For all you know, Ted of Ted and Ed, I could have a fleet of Mercury cars and out here, a flotilla of Buicks and Cadillacs, big cars like ovens, cruise 'round this campus in a funeral procession, a nun stationed in each car, riding shotgun."

"Oolong. What's your real name? I forgot it."

"I don't have a name."

"Swell. Get in."

They went, College Drive, Route 19a, 16, the Mass. Pike, into Cambridge in the red motor car, Oolong had a hand on the door handle and one on the dashboard. She had never seen a car this small go that fast, but she didn't want to say anything, appear chicken.

"I'm scaring you, aren't I?"

"I've never been in a car before."

They parked the car ("Say it: They pocked the caa; you say it just like them. I've never heard it so good.") somewhere on one of those little streets in Cambridge; he locked the car. "I can't take you into my room now," Ted said; "it's not the time yet."

"What makes you think," she said in a high voice, "I want to go into your room; I don't."

"That's what they all say."

"Who all?"

"Never mind."

Now Ted, all white and blue, sounded nervous; he didn't sound like himself, subway Ted, hotdog Ted; it was getting quiet and awkward. "What do you want to do instead?"

"Why don't you show me this Harvard. I'd like to see it."

They had reached Harvard Square and Ted (whose real name was

Matt, not Michael, although he was perfectly happy with Ted) took out a pair of black mittens. "Do you like these?" Yes. "Then, I'll just put them on. If I put them on, maybe you'll put your glove in this mitten?

"Then I'll show you Harvard, but don't try to infiltrate the premises, sneak some of the nuns down, elect another Catholic president, you and your popes; keep your mumbo jumbo at a distance."

They went in and out, up and down, here and there; they saw this and that, ate a hot fudge sundae and a package of Milkduds. He said: "Long Island, New York, 1955." You're younger than I am. "I know. I'm younger than everybody." Schools, brothers and sisters, vacation in Europe and one in Mexico City, "and now . . ." Now what? "Now I'm here with Oolong, *in saecula saeculorum*, amen." How do you know that?

She said: Praav-Dintz.

"What part of Russia is that in?" He took his hand out of her hand, took out a skinny notepad, turned her around and wrote on her back. "See." On the notepad was Провидэнц. "That's what you said." I didn't say that. "You said that." This made it all seem silly.

⟡ Oolong Kane went back to Christ College that night, too late for supper. I have had, she told Rickee, who was jumping on the bed and off the bed, hugging Roomie and skittering about, whooping and laughing, my first date with a real boy. I may look a mess now, she told Rickee, turning to the mirror: streaky face, heavy circles, flattened hair, glittery eyes, but I was—. "Roomie!!" Rickee circled the room again, leaping from bed to bed. She took Roomie Oolong to the talk room, Barbara's bedroom, full of snacks and pretty lampshades, perfumes and throw rugs, and after a half hour of talk about the real date with the real boy, and seeing all those eager faces, scrubbed clean for the night and one of them trying to learn German verbs but not miss any of the interesting parts, told them Anne Marie had done it.

This was wonderful. This was a relief. They were all, in their own way, getting closer and closer to doing it, step by step, inch by inch, and Anne Marie was nowhere near: Honor thy father and mother; thou shalt not kill; thou shalt not commit adultery; so this put her way ahead and out of reach, so she could slow down and listen to the stories and not have to hear them thinking: backward, retard, old-fashioned, asexual, up-tight, nunny, untouched, spinsterish, cold, immature, prissy, and frigid. They were egging her on—Margaret and Barbara, especially—both at the brink themselves, with boy-friends at Worcester Tech and the Berklee School of Music, apart-ments of their own and cars, and it was just a matter of time, every-body knew, but Mags and Bags, as they were called, were spacing it all out, the kisses and strokes, the over the clothes and under the clothes, the rubs and inserts; they were dragging it out as they were brought closer to the goal, and it was fun. Now, someone was there, planted a flag, Christ College, class of 1975, and all in one night, square into a squealing, flailing son of Harvard.

It was a triumph and Mags still had the bottle of peppermint schnapps she had bought for the fun of it in Boston, and they drank capfuls as the story got thicker with details, moves and counter-moves. It was late in the story—the story had been going on for three-quarters of an hour and the group had been told to pipe down a couple of times—when something shifted and Mags and Bags, more familiar with the subject than O.K., began taking it over with questions and cross-questions that were weakening the facts, mak-ing them seem less realistic. Bags suddenly remembered, lighting an illegal Marlboro from the tip of one of Mags', while Rickee was spraying the cracks around the door with air freshener: "Hey, Anne Marie Kane, come on. You don't even use a tampon; it must have hurt like hell."

This pain, which Miss Kane had not calculated into the story, was, yes, a needed, but an unwanted detail, would throw off the lav-ish, rich sense of it, the careful rise and fall, the control and mastery, so she resisted by battering back with new details about sneaking through the basement of Kenilworth Hall, hand by hand, with the help of Ted's friends, a mystery tour, so dark you couldn't see any-thing, and scary.

But there was something different in their faces. The faces were turning from a concentrated gape to something slack, as the cred-ibility drained out of the story. "Come on," Bags said, passing the lit cigarette to O. K., who took a puff, "admit it. You might have done something, but you"—a big excitement was gathering again at the thought of a story that wasn't true—"of all people"—Mags chimed in, and they all chimed in—"DIDN'T GO ALL the WAY!"

Everyone was screaming. The air was cleared. The story was just as good untrue. It was better; now, it was still coming toward all of them and no one among them was going to take all the joy out of it, and leave everyone behind late.

And O.K. still had the hidden story that nobody knew: that Matt

Michael had given her a kiss near the dark Charles River, a kiss on the lips, and another one on freezing cold lips, but thrilling enough. Thrilling enough to give everyone the wrong idea: not the first time that had happened.

And there were to be more nights and days away. "Anne Marie Kane, you have a visitor," and "Anne Marie Kane has a caller." "Anne Marie Kane." Sometimes in the red car ("Anne Marie Kane") and sometimes on the subway. It didn't matter. She would always ("Anne Marie Kane") go with him, and be glad to go.

❧ Instead, Oolong died one night, a flash in the pan, and went to heaven a virgin. In the days that followed, a skull rolled out and went forward, rolled down and out. The skull, an A student, 165 pounds gained overnight and all of it arranged like a corky inner tube around its middle earth, received no calls from Cambridge, no calls came for the skull. The Michael Fury, so tender-hearted and mirthful, so genial and supple-witted, had his own eggs to fry in his home ground, and the old egg up-country could rot and coo in its web of nuns and its cell of cement and fiberglass curtains, the daily walks to the food hall, the feel of wire rollers crowning the skull's skull with nightly thorns, for its disappointment. How did the skull know before he didn't call, Ted, Matt, or Michael, that he wouldn't? Because the skull's life wasn't ready to fold up its bony lakes and plates, islands and pools, into something perfect. It, the skull, was still too imperfect: its plates all cracked and overlapped, different plates from different eras, some plastic, some glass, little and big, hollowed and flat. It wasn't even moving, it was stalled, dead; so go away, cloudlike thing from Harvard, beautiful blue pitcher.

This skull, Ka, rolled for a year in its circuit of classes, its round of dinners, its clatter of trips home and trips back, its room with Rickee, a skull hatch, a serene home for skulls, until one day, the hard brittle ball, by now a know-it-all, a brain, an authority, rolled out to the mailbox on the sidewalk just outside, and dropped an envelope in: To Harvard. Let me in. Signed, The Skull. And it did. The skull brushed its hard skull and cloaked itself, bone and gristle, with drapes and rags and rolled in from its Russian city, Провидэнц, with the help of the skull's new and false beau, Dr. Mark Smith, M.D., whom the skull met as a skull, nothing more, because Smith was himself a skull, earth-colored, no lips, tunnels for eyes. This was the skull's inamorato and the amor took place on a metal bed with a thin medical towel as a pad and a follow-up of peanut-butter sandwiches, which the double skulls slapped right on their heads. Hence, the skull that replaced the Oolong rolled to the Harvard ground already defiled and set for the next twenty years. Signed: The Skull, and it did.

SOLITAIRE

is a French word. And for my examination I will cut it in three:
so lit aire, so there will be a bed for me to lie on when I'm
finished.

When I place it there, centered and alone, yet tie it to "is a
French word," I'm asking forebearance. How final is this exam?
How final is anything if it can be grabbed and thrown down the
sewer? I never lie to myself if lie mean be exhaustive, talk in an exhausted tone.

I ask the question what is solitaire? That solitaire has a bed
and I lie on it and no place to play cards lying down.

The workaday word, every world has the three parts from
which the desired object (lit) can be extracted, but not with a
sharp object, or anything metal. This has already been said, but
neither like a nut in a nutshell, or a mental case called vegetable,
one of the things an extracter once objected to in an earlier examination, but this was another lie because part of the question was
already covered in a still earlier exam: your son is mental, your father is dead.

The question cannot be reversed: French word is a solitaire?
although in that the skirt is lifted up and the pants pulled down.

When will I get to the point? It is not a point at all, but a plane
with a corpus on it, although not being a liar, I have to say dead
to myself, not dead to you; otherwise no examination, no resting
place.

But can it move faster? This is too slow; other things move
too, and the distance will not be covered unless certain things
can be left behind for good, and then exhausted, climb up on the
bed.

Fourthly, night comes and other things with it. My answers
will not have any // through them, nor will I use—; the word will
be separated by a plunging motion until places are sucked between
the parts and nothing you can do about it.

At the break I'll get up with the rest and smoke a cigarette,
go to the lavatory.

Don't expect the extreme transformation, for it is just the first
part of a longer project like anything else. It is a mere diagram

now, if you will take these fragile pieces into your hand—that is the romance of it. Later comes the civitas dei with all its sites and spaces.

Please come over right now and look. See the dancing man, see the dancing feet. See the rods between.

Pick these tiny pieces up into your hands. The slat and the foot and the head, but no lively cincture, no dancing integument. Nothing but this bed. I will act out the rest of the puzzle and take these five minutes to do it. Solitaire is a French word and there is also in there a bed.

EFORE, though, it spent its last summer at home, in its square home with the Kanes, Al and Marie, Jimmy and Ellen, and the grandmother; the house was the same, the car was the same, and the skull sat in the back and was whisked around with airs whirling and streaming through its teeth. There was a comfort to it. If they were the same, grouchy, mean, and sarcastic, yelling at the same small deviations like shutting the venetian blinds so the slats went the wrong way; preoccupied with the same clamorous activity: Sunday outings and Sunday dinners, Sunday Mass and Sunday bakeries, attacking and buzzing at each other, and selecting the precise irritating word to rub in and keep rubbing; saying the same words, having the same expression on their face, eating the same food, getting up at the same time, going out of the same door, parking the same car in the same spot; even the same old squawking bluejay arrowing across the lawn, barking at the cat, who could catch every other kind of bird but this; the same oil patch on the driveway, and narrow yellow pathway through the grass: don't walk on the grass, Goddamn it, then it, the skull, was, by analogy or by something—if you could speak so simply about it—ditto. This couldn't be true after all that had happened, but the skull was tempted by it, as the Kanes recognized nothing of difference; so go ahead, fall back on your old ways; or, be different and see if anyone even notices. It was a nice bath of mental neutrality, and so easy now to be cut into in a familiar way, to smile a dull smile and roll over. To go back to sleep on the old nails, tacks—they were more like tacks.

The more trouble the pre-skull had gotten into at college, and the sadder and more twisted it was, the less the family was interested. Tell us the good parts, Marie was forever telling her daughter; save these dreary things—I don't even get half of what you're telling me; I never went through any of this and neither did your father; I've never heard of it before; are you sure you're not making it up?—for someone your own age.

They were in the bathroom, the skull sitting on the edge of the tub while Marie was washing her face with a facecloth, over a sinkful of sudsy water, slightly tinted with makeup. She twisted her neck slightly to look at Anne Marie with squinty eyes, then went back to the facecloth, and, as the question wasn't answered, and the request not met, changed the subject.

A lot of pressure: verbal and ocular, was put on the skull during this time to feed its tight bones: how are you going to go through all your troubles if you don't eat? But, no one in this house ate: they pretended to eat, but they didn't really eat. If something passed through the brittle wall of the teeth and was not rejected by a quick squeeze of the throat: reviled and repelled, these metal balls and screws, tinsoldiers, pennies and ballpoint fillers; if something snuck through and dropped down, it was only to wreak havoc down there: burn a path, roil and broil; more an adventure than an ingestion; so, even in this, the skull was at home being at home.

It was fun. The skull took a walk every single day past all the familiar things, stores, holes in the sidewalk, tired trees, branch library with its smell of glue and pencils, tiny houses and alleys, church, schoolyard; it was all exactly the same, but more faded looking.

One night, Mary L. Conley, a stranger, still mad at Anne Marie Kane, traitor and anti-cleric, heresiarch, alien, drug addict (drug addict? The word had gotten around: Anne Marie Kane, always far out, was frequenting with drugs, and not drugs from the drugstore: oreomyocin, capsules and cough syrups, poultices and ace bandages, Ben Gay and St. Joseph's orange aspirins, calomine lotion and coke syrup, Mercurochrome, Bromo Seltzer and Kaopectate), and also pregnant. Am I pregnant, too? the skull said over the old black telephone, out in the open so everyone could hear; Miss Conley didn't answer: if the former Anne M. Kane were going to mock her for being in Providence, let her go ahead; called her former friend, out-of-state, home on vacation, to see if she would like to go out of a Saturday with a group of friends from the teachers' college, all teacher's ed, soon to be teachers in the public schools—do you want to make something of it? Yes.

The skull hung up the old phone and received questions: Where, what, why was it happening and what did it mean? A row of questions (Marie, Al and Ellen were sitting at the supper table when the call had come) followed by a second row. And how is Mary Conley? How's her family? Does she like college? Is she doing what you're doing? Does she have a boyfriend yet? Is she still living at home? They knew the answers to these questions because they saw the Conleys: Mrs., Elizabeth, and Mary L. every Sunday at the eleven o'clock Mass; Mr. Conley, a baker for longer than anyone could remember, was deceased: the whole Kane family had gone to the wake and still remembered every detail. But they also knew, the skull knew they knew, every detail of the life of Mary L. Conley: if she had gained a boyfriend, they would be able to see it, or it would be on the avenue picking up something at the A&P or the package store, or Elizabeth would have mentioned it when Mrs. Kane saw her on the bus going downtown every morning: And how's Mary? How does she like school? So, the answers the skull had available—and she didn't have many—were superfluous, there simply for the pleasure of the family, hearing once more what it already knew.

The skull opened and a tiny girl emerged much refreshed with the prospect of a night spent with the very rich hours of Miss Mary Conley, a wit and a good-time Charlie. The girl arranged her thoughts for this: she wanted to sit this Mary down with her pleasant pink face and pale eyes, a face people called the map of Ireland, and sit across from it, unfold these thousand stories with their inroads and incrustations, the undertones, the pain, the purple scenes, the spurs and balls, the mortifications and then they could both laugh and mock at all the fools and pharisees, the familiar types they had mocked all the way through high school, a gallery of local jerks and marks, but good enough to sharpen their wits on, and to ease Miss Conley of her bellyful of acid remarks and critical comments. The idea of this night made the girl fall backwards onto the twin bed with a low bounce and satisfying sigh. But not for long, for someone was coming up the stairs.

❧ Mary C's eyes were made up with blue and violet eye powders, with a heavy ring around the eyes and under the eyelashes. Her pale face was very pale, but shaded in with brownish rouge, her hair was in a million perfect curls and bounced as she walked in, a big stretchy smile for Mr. and Mrs. Kane, Jimmy, Ellen and the grandmother, who were all right there to meet her. "Hello, Mrs. Kane, Mr. Kane, hi there Mrs. Rowley, Ellen, Jimmy." Hi Mary, hi Mary. Hello there, dearie. How do you do, sister; how's your mother? Fine, good, and Elizabeth? Mary Conley said they were all fine. Mr. Kane had gotten her a chair so she could sit and visit a minute with them. And what will you have? Can I offer you—? "Nothing for me, thanks," said the Miss Conley, "my mother just made such a dinner."

The room was full of sighs. Mary Conley's mother, Mrs. John F. Conley, was famous for dinner, for cooking, for baking and broiling two or three kinds of meat, potatoes and rice, several vegetables, pie and cake, rolls from the bakery, apple sauce and chutney, pickles and relish, milk and ales, ice cream and cookies, port and brandy and pure Irish linen napkins and tablecloth. Miss Kane loved to eat there and put the pretty lace napkin on her lap and pick whatever she wanted from the thick array of hot and cold dishes. Mrs. Conley, pleasant-enough talking but grim-faced, jumped up every minute to get something fresh, to take away something, to bring more. Miss Kane had never seen her without her apron. She wore white tennis shoes to move quickly, soundlessly, from pantry to kitchen, but she also wore them, Mary Conley had said, but it might have been just a story, because she loved the Celtics. These weren't hightops, though, the dogged Anne M. insisted. True, Conley said, but they slap the floor, free shot, lay-up, pivots and one-on-one just like. Get out. No, you get out. Mrs. Conley was often silent, lips tight and face closed, but when she let out a remark, it was funny and, although the farthest she got into the world was to the A&P on Chalkstone and back, she was very up-to-the-minute: she watched a lot of talk shows and read the morning and evening papers, *Saturday Review, Time* and *Life, Commonweal, The Messenger of the Blind, The Boston Pilot, Catholic Week* and the *Reader's Digest.* When she cooked, which was all the time, she listened to the call-in shows on local radio until Elizabeth bought her a shortwave radio and she listened to the New York and Chicago talk shows, much better, she said, much more interesting, real talkers, live wires and intellectuals, sometimes wackos called in on these shows, not just the everyday person with a glass to the wall, or a party line to listen in on—the ones everyone in Providence knew, planted next to their windows day and night, spying.

So, we can't fix you anything, Mr. Kane, eager, asked again. No, no thanks, Mr. Kane, I'm just fine. Miss Conley twisted around to look at Anne Marie, standing there, paralyzed and gaping. "Hi there, A.M., I didn't even see you. You got your hair cut."

Anne Marie felt for her hair; it was still there, although for Conley's sharp gaze, it might not be. There was a mutual inspection to do, but now wasn't the time to do it, so Miss C. shifted back to the family. They had followed her eyes to Anne Marie, and now back again. So, how's your mother? Miss Conley took a small photograph from her purse, a picture of her brother Henry's new baby, Charlie: Charles Christopher Conley. The family took the picture. Miss Conley, her face all rosy and beaming, also offered them a few stories about people they knew: Teresa Archiolli, who had a little private money and was in thick with the priests, embroidered linens for the altar and ran a million errands for the church, who kept the two yipping toy poodles in the tiny apartment over McCarthy's, was now, to keep her hair sleek and fluffy like a girl's, giving it a bath of eggs and mayonnaise once a week. Get out, Ellen Kane said. "She *is;* she told Elizabeth one night. Elizabeth called her up to go downtown shopping. 'I can't,' Teresa said, 'my hair's all dripping with eggs and mayonnaise.'" Miss Conley threw back her head and let out a yelp of helpless sounding laughter. Around this laugh, there was a silence. The Kanes didn't get it.

It wasn't so much funny, Mrs. Kane said to her husband later on when he was sitting paging through the evening paper again, to check if he'd missed any tidbits, and drinking his bedtime coffee milk with the cookies on the napkin, as weird, didn't you think? I never liked that Teresa Archiolli, Mrs. Kane went on, her back to Mr. Kane, leaving the room, not only is she weird, but I don't like those yippy dogs either; I wonder why she has them; they can't be giving her that much company.

Listen, Mr. Kane told her, shaking the papers, I don't even know the woman. Why are you telling *me?*

Mrs. Kane came back into the room. How do you think Mary Conley looked? I thought she looked much better than last time. There's a little color in her face and she fixed herself up so nice. I wouldn't be surprised if she doesn't have a boyfriend.

I wouldn't know, came the voice behind the paper. She say anything about her family?

I can't remember.

Nice family—I like the mother.

I think she looks better than Annie. I think Annie looks kind of punk, what do you think? Do you think she looks kind of punk?

I don't know. Don't ask me so many questions. I looked at the girl. She looks fine. Why don't you get off her back?

I'm not on her back. I was just making a simple statement. Mrs. Kane drifted out again. At the door: Geez, you can't even say anything around here without you barking.

I'm not barking. Did you hear me barking? (Marie Kane was heading up the stairs and put her hands on her ears. He was swearing down there, and let him.) Mrs. Kane slipped into Ellen's room, which the girl now had to share with poison, so moved all her stuff as far away as she could from the twin bed so designated. Ellen was all around the rim of the room under the two small windows. Her mother came in and planked herself down on HER bed. "How do you think she looks? I was just asking your father, but he had to go and work himself all up."

Who?

"You know who," Mrs. K. pointed to the bed she was sitting on. Oh, her. I don't know; don't ask me.

"Well who am I going to ask? I already asked him. No one wants to talk to me. Anne Marie, at least, will talk to me; none of the rest of you will." Mrs. K. drifted out and circled around, went downstairs and finally settled in her own chair in front of the TV and picked up a section of the paper she found on the floor: sports; she wasn't interested in sports, so she put it down, got up, turned the TV on. "I kind of miss her, you know. I'm glad she came home."

What?

"I *said*—. Oh, never mind."

I heard you, Marie. You miss her; you're glad she's home. Well, I'm glad you're happy, that's all. He shook the sheets of paper again in a little rage, a beginning rage. Well, I don't think she looks so great myself, he said, for a young woman that age. She has no color in her face, her skin is bad. What's wrong with her skin? I never had trouble with my skin, and you didn't either.

"Oh I had my troubles and so did my sisters."

Well, not like *that*.

"I don't think we should be running her down."

I'm not running her down. Who says I'm running her down! You wanted to talk. Why'd you ask me?

"Your father's," Mary Conley was saying as she backed her sister's car, Chevy Impala, out of the Kane driveway, "a hot sketch. So's your mother, but your father's really a card." By this, and by the tight look on Mary's face, Anne Marie could tell she didn't want to get into anything too personal right away. They could warm up for a while on the neighbors, on the local scene, if Anne Marie Kane, Christ College, Boston, hadn't forgotten it. To prove she hadn't, Anne Marie, her hands in tight balls on her lap, asked a big jumbled question, and all the way down Chalkstone, through downtown, and onto the southeast expressway, they talked about this one and that one. This one had gone into the convent, but not before making a big hullaballoo about—you're not going to believe this, Anne Mary (Mary L. was using the nuns' ready conversion for what they took as a name veering a little to the pagan, a little on the dangerously ornamental side)—underwear. Get out. Cross my heart and hope to die.

Their two old girlfriends, Paula and Mary Ann, with a vocation since Grade 1 and long overdue, planned to enter September of the year Miss Kane went to Christ and Mary Conley to R.I.U. They were all set by senior year and had special meetings with several of the older nuns to gather the right things together and discard the wrong things and start buying new things. The word was to "discard" or pass down all brassières ("Is that what they called them?" Miss Kane asked Mary L.) because they wouldn't be in use. ("They wouldn't be 'in use'! What does that mean?") It meant, and Mary L. with Paula, and later with Anne Mary, discussed this in fine; they'd be wearing something else. ("What?") I don't know: undershirts probably. This idea of undershirts caused a little furor among the girls (Mary L., Anne Mary, Josephine, Eleanor, Jane, Cynthia, and Martina) who knew Paula Mahan, but no furor at all around the friendless and content-just-to-be-a-nun-and-get-it-over-with Mary Frances Maloney, who liked the idea. She had an aunt a nun and it was fine with her, no matter what they did. The stranger the better; the more it made them different, the better: that was the idea, wasn't it? The second half of senior year, when they all had to get through college entrance, senior prom, May procession, graduation, and other ordeals, Paula Mahan had to get over the idea of an undershirt, and she had gotten over it by conferences with the practical Mary Conley, who finally said, after deep inhalation through the teeth, many jokes, many moments of revulsion and moments of titillation, who cares? What difference does it make? No one will know but you.

This worked for a month, but the problem came back later. Paula Mahan couldn't get used to the idea. She had argued a little with old Mother Maria Conception, who said: dearie, don't give it another thought, which didn't mean: relax, it's all taken care of; it meant: don't bring it up again, case closed. But, Mary Conley explained, driving in her usual way—little spurts of speed, followed by slowing down; jerking down the highway, sometimes over the speed limit, sometimes well below—it was a whole new ballgame now. "How come?" The nuns, their old order straight from Ireland, were in the process, she said, of revamping their outfits in line with Vatican II. The old habit, even for the full-blown, Golden Jubilee nuns, was out; the new habit, blue skirt, white blouse, jerkin, little veil with hair showing, stockings and old lady pumps, was in. Now, Mary L. went on, you can't wear one of those light cotton blouses—excuse *me*— *they* can't wear one of those light blouses without the protection of a full slip and, as Paula says they're called—I talked to her just last week from Canada—a foundation.

"A foundation?"

Yup, so out goes all the old undershirts. A new era, a new regime. "Is Paula relieved?"

She says it doesn't matter. There are other things worse wrong. They talked about how political the nuns were, how everything was hush-hush, but mountains were moved on a particular someone's say-so, while someone else could talk to the wall for all the good it did; plus, there was a lot of bickering and petty disputes: you wouldn't believe it. But I'm not surprised; they're just people—worse, they're women and all cooped up together. Yet, Mary L. said, slapping the steering wheel and causing the car to jump a little off course, she's still—she turned to look Anne Marie in the face—she's still trying to talk me into going in with her. Anne Marie laughed. "What do you tell her?" I tell her that God Almighty would have to come down on his broomstick first. To get me.

Good, Anne Marie said.

"Good, nothing," Mary L. snapped back, "I wouldn't go where you are either. Your life—I can tell by looking at you; I wouldn't have to read your tearjerking letters, which I like to read; don't get me wrong—is no bed of roses, sister. In a lot of ways," she was looking now for the exit; Anne Marie had no idea where exactly they were going; "I'd go to the Motherhouse first. At least you know what you're getting into there."

They were on the exit ramp. "Do you think I look bad?" Anne Marie said in a small voice. I'm not criticizing you, the driver said; far be it from me to criticize someone with your brain, but yes, you look like someone's been draining your blood. I thought—they were on a little expressway now, Route 2, heading south—I admit it, you'd come back with a Boston accent and a thousand little ways, but you're exactly the same. "Thanks."

Big deal. Maybe you *should* change. If you get the chance to get out, maybe you should go and mix with them. Who am I to say, but it doesn't seem, from what you've told me, you're doing that either. You're—she made a left into a big parking lot next to a white clapboard house, huge, with a piazza and people on it, drinking and talking and smoking, making a big racket—letting them walk all over you. I wouldn't let them, if I were you. Who do they think they are?

Anne Marie didn't know exactly who this "they" was; it could be anybody. Mary Conley turned the ignition off, but looked straight ahead. "Don't let yourself be a doormat, Anne Marie; it's you who's doing it. You're the one that lets people treat you like dirt. You must like it."

Anne Marie said she didn't like it. That's why she was transfer-
ring—to get out, to get to someplace better.

Worse, Mary L. said.

Better, Anne K. said.

"Worse." They were laughing. "Listen," Mary said; "what do I
know about any of this; where am I in life that I should tell you what
to do? Don't listen to me."

⏺ But Anne Marie, brand-new transfer student to Harvard University, or Hahvid, as it was called, and people loved calling it; and mys-
tified as to what to bring with her this time in her suitcase, *did* listen.
Miss Conley had a lot to say and she said it. It was a relief to listen to
her saying it. Anne Marie didn't even need to unwrap and unroll the
thousand nested stories; Miss Conley took care of it all with a few
stories of her own and the large designs she saw in these stories. It
was taken care of in a few weeks: Anne Marie would refer her back
to the topic when she felt she needed it, and Miss Conley, with a
growing outrage and desire to slander and judge, would come at it
from another angle, leaving all the villains, mockers, taunters, and
hideous enemies a pile of rubble, with only one problem. If it was all
bad, and it had always been bad, where was the good of it?

Miss Kane knew she had felt the good of it, but the good of the
Conley wrecking ball was to bring it all down; she couldn't do it and
leave just the second floor dressing room where all the new clothes
were, or the preparations for dates and the Saturday morning trip to
Boston on the MTA and all the delicious sundaes and beautiful dark
roads of Massachusetts. This would not stand alone in the air, and
this was attached to so many other things, days and complicated
events that Anne Marie had to keep a whole mental neighborhood of
the past a secret from the kind but dangerous solace of Mary L. Conley. Too bad, because some of these sections: sooty and narrow, gar-
bage-strewn streets, needed airing out.

But talk of these awful towns and their demolition was only part
of the summer works of Conley and Kane. Conley, primary ed, had
drawn around herself a group of new friends, boys and girls, all from
Rhode Island and mostly from Providence, who knew, Miss C. had
said that night in the car, exactly how to have a good time and keep
having it. Miss Conley had never known how to have a good time,
and had never wanted one. Sometimes, when they were in high
school, and you might hear of a good time indirectly, or overhear
directly when they would stand side-by-side in the basement of their

high school, an old office building; and in the damp basement with painted wooden tables, after buying a pint of milk or a large bottle of Coke from the nuns, eat a bag lunch: egg salad, peanut butter, apple, three cookies—one of the nuns liked to stand near them and talk to them, so mostly they didn't overhear much; that Alberta Pellegrino, Nancy Sawyer, and Linda Testa, three especially cute girls and inseparable, who went with three friends at LaSalle Academy, had been known of a Friday night to go to the show or out for a clam roll with Frank D., Larry A. and John L., drink a little beer or a rum with coke, if they could get it, and park on River Road. River Road was something Anne Marie could not get Mary Conley to talk or think about. She wasn't that interested in boys, and boys weren't that interested in her; except that, being a hot ticket, she sometimes made them laugh, if she could get within earshot to do it. Only once had Anne Marie been able to talk the reluctant and sensitive, the testy and sarcastic Mary Conley into attending a Friday night canteen at LaSalle. They dressed alike: skirt, sweater, and stood in a packed line for half an hour in the cold, and then herded in (as M.L.C. described it later a million times until A.M.K. couldn't stand to hear it anymore. "Well, don't ask me," Mary said blandly, "to go again then, if you don't want to hear about it.") by some of the Christian brothers on duty for that night, and up the stairs to the auditorium where they paid their dollar, were stamped on the hand and allowed to enter, only to stand on their legs (now A.M. couldn't recall it herself without hearing the grouchy tones of her friend, exaggerating, dismissing) with a thousand high school girls in a big clump, and hope some jacket and tie might knife through this still crowd of skirts and sweaters and tight faces till he arrived dead center at Kane and Conley—who did not stand out, just the opposite—and say— what did they say?—May I have this dance? no. Wannadance? or, Yuhwannadance? in a mumble, and then have to paw and bump against this crowd to arrive at the edge of the dance floor where the couples were bouncing and jerking in solemn ones, or slumped on each other and shuffling their feet an inch here, an inch back. For that, Miss Conley was known to say and then repeat it, I want to stand in a crowd of snobs from St. X's and Bay View (the high schools for girls whose parents had moved them to the suburbs, or at least, to the nicer sections of Providence) until my feet are ready to fall off and you won't even talk to me, so busy you are eyeballing the area, and what good does it do you, you can't even see anything without your glasses, Anne Marie; when no one's going to ask the likes of us to dance.

Anne Marie thought this was unfair: it could happen that someone would ask them to dance, plus it was a very exciting night anyway. You could march around the corridor of the high school, and boys would do this too; or you could go upstairs to the place where they sold the Cokes, a classroom, and boys in there, sit in there a while. The trick was, Anne Marie knew this but wasn't sure Mary L. did; she didn't like to think any further than she had to; to dance with a boy more than once, be talking so smoothly at the end of the song that another song would start up and you'd still be holding hands, instead of having the boy turn on his heel, see ya, or say nothing at all, just turn on his heel, and from two dances to an invitation to walk up the stairs to the Coke room and have a Coke bought, and sit down at a desk with a boy of your own so people (people like you and me, high and dry and bored, Mary L. would say) could see you. Was this it?

☙ It was that first night out that Anne Marie could see Mary L. Conley had changed her ways. She didn't look like herself: thin, no makeup, just the gleaming map, anymore; she was more glamorous, and the map disguised by new hair and makeup. Under an ordinary cardigan buttoned up while she sat at the kitchen table of the Kanes was a thin, black knit dress with a straight skirt, a nice dress which made Mary L. Conley's pretty white face look less white. The reddish brown curls were all shiny in the bar lights, a long bar with small tables and a bandstand, crowded everywhere, lively, and people pushing to get drinks and get seats at a table. Miss Conley was drinking her third whiskey sour, telling funny and funnier stories to her group of R.I. classmates, all primped up like Mary L. in cocktail dresses and jackets, pink and white faces and smooth hair, elaborately made-up blue eyes. Mary L. was funnier and more brutal than she had ever been in her life and you could hear her laughing all through the bar, and people laughing. This group, Anne Marie could see, was different looking from the people she had seen at Christ, older-looking, dressing more like her mother's friends going out for an evening to a nightclub, drinking and smoking and talking about politics, the beach, and school teaching. After a while, Mary L. Conley stopped telling stories and the group broke up a little; the jukebox music ended and a little band: accordian, guitar, and bagpipes, started playing. Anne Marie stayed exactly where she was, right at the elbow of Miss Conley, listening to the music, but at the other elbow was the first in a series of men standing up at the bar, who had found their way to the palavering girl in black at the big table. These men—there must have been at least three—tried to meet Mary Conley during that one night, get her phone number or talk her into coming back at a pre-arranged time to the Rooster; they didn't look like college boys, but Mary L. was nice to them anyways, joked and abused, said this is a friend of mine from Boston, and pointed an upturned hand at Anne Marie Kane, sweater and skirt, and talked more, then got up to go to the ladies' room, Anne Marie following close behind, and stayed there long enough so the latest stag would return to his spot at the bar and Mary L. could re-settle with a fresh pack of cigarettes, Old Golds, and a new drink, and the table become lively again.

There was dancing to the Irish band, who played all recognizable tunes; certain of Mary L.'s friends got up and danced a jig or reel with their little fingers raised and linked together. Mary L. and Anne M. watched these dances. "I hate Irish dancing," Anne Marie whispered to Mary Conley, who looked her in the face. "Why?" "I'm sick of it." "Why? It's not like it was with the nuns."

"It's exactly like that," Miss Kane said with a sour tone, "what's the difference?"

"If you can't see it, I can't explain it to you."

Anne Marie was sorry she had insulted the dancing; Mary L. C. was easily insulted, and sure enough, she looked sad.

The dancing was followed by a piano playing Irish songs and people singing the songs in a big group. Miss Kane didn't want to sing these. Some people had moved up to the piano. Everyone was sentimental and the voices were sentimental. Anne Marie couldn't stand it; she didn't understand why this stuff was better now after it had been so tedious in grammar school, when they had to sing these songs, "Have You Ever Been Across the Sea to Ireland," "My Wild Irish Rose," "Mary," H-A-double R-I (her father sang this song all the time) every year at the St. Patrick's day play and at Christmas standing before an audience of one: the pastor, who loved these songs; and also for the St. Patrick's Day parade, marching down Regent Avenue, white and green. Why did kids want to sing these old songs at a bar now that they were away from the nuns and grown up?

Anne Marie Kane, quiet and unfriendly, was never called back for a night at the White Rooster and there were lots of nights that summer. Mary Conley and Anne Marie were still friends, but they went out, when they went out at all, just the two of them, to a movie or to a bar on the East Side near Brown.

"This," Mary Conley said, after she'd driven Anne Marie to Briggs Spa on Waterman, without a word of explanation, and pulled the key out of the ignition to stare out the windshield, "is more your speed, right?"

They ordered glasses of wine in Briggs: all students, all Brown, all talking, all snooty—it was like being at a canteen again; they were completely ignored, so they talked to each other. It was friendly, at least it seemed friendly; but it was different. Mary Conley was showing her exactly how much she had made a kind of bed for herself,and now just lie in it, why complain. By the end of the summer, Mary L. was busy with a steady date, a chef from Newport, who played rugby; as handsome a man—Anne Marie's parents, Al and Marie, saw this man at the Rooster; they and their friends liked to go to the Rooster, too—as you could hope to see, and that Mary Conley, boy has she changed, out there raising hell. I hope, Mrs. K. added, that girl doesn't have to drive herself home after a night like that.

Mary L. had made a point of visiting the Kane table to say hi, how do, and had made a hilarious but cutting remark to Anne Marie's own loudmouth Uncle Ed, full of himself he was, and had tried to give Mary L. a hug and a squeeze. "That set him back, I tell you," Mrs. Kane said, "and it was good for him." She had never seen big Uncle Ed at a loss for words, and he never forgot it either; but always asked after that little pipsqueak Conley with the mouth; but looked forward to meeting her again, which he did; and it happened again.

Marie Kane told her daughter that she heard big Uncle Ed tell Frannie Doorley, a neighbor, recent widower, quiet, friends with everyone, although his voice box removed and never bothered to hook up the machinery hanging on his chest so he could talk, that that little girl wouldn't live to see her thirtieth birthday with all her teeth intact.

Anne Marie was surprised at this, even though she knew the girl and knew what she could say given half a chance and the right provocation: Mary L. had let one of the nuns have it, too, for accusing her of a lapse in judgment which led to a funny item being included in the class will: We the class of 1971, St. Edward's High School, being of sound mind and body, leave to Mother Transfigurata our beanies and senior ties, for her to supply the ranks of seniors to follow, who lose and abuse them, who cut them in half and dribble down food, and let them blow and roll down Exeter Street, gone forever; or just forget them, and have to bobbypin a hankie or Kleenex to their heads in front of the Blessed Sacrament.

It was stupid, yes, and yes, the nuns were not supposed to be mentioned anywhere in sport, never, they knew that; or in public, and not singled out like that, yes, they knew that—many people heard it the day the livid Transfigurata, or Figaro, as they called her, bellowed at Mary L. Conley in room 1 right near the windows, while they were at recreation in the parking lot; but they heard it even better, a lot of red faces and smiles of surprise, rounded eyes of amazement, when the voice of Mary L. Conley, hero, bellowed back even louder, surrounding the nun's angry shrill with shriller and harsher: "How dare you accuse me," breath was held from Exeter to Dover Street, the world stood still while a tone was used on a nun, a holy woman, "Mother Transfigurata, you who boast to us every day in Religion 302, of a finer self and a higher calling—" Miss Kane, her eyes rolling up to Heaven, rested her back on the brick wall of St. Edward's High School as she heard the unmistakeable waiver in the voice of Mary L. Conley, flexing this voice for what would be a long and well-orated self-defense and acid bath: the nun would never live it down, she was sure, and Mary L. would die in the Vatican Brig, a prisoner of blasphemous invective; life sentence, loss of tongue, blinding, quartering, flattening, evisceration, excommunication, flight into Egypt, thou shalt not take the name of the Lord thy God in vain; and it was happening and let it: "who prate constantly of the need to examine oneself before judging the world, to be above self-importance and self-justification, to understand first, to be compassionate, never self-righteous or smug in our deserts, to well up in fellow feeling and shrink in the self and its prerogatives, to fill the soul with grace, not contumely; with fullness, not niggardly measure; universal love, not pettiness. Here you are, our ideal, the one we look to, without equal, for an example, engorged with petty anger and bursting with unjust accusations, taking not a minute out of your rage to examine your own conscience, let alone consider the case in question from any angle other than your own inflated pride and self esteem."

The nun was still shrieking with pain, but the tone was dying down, as Miss Conley's greater virtuosity was demanding more and more of her attention; she had to remember, Miss Kane figured, what was being said to her so she could force Miss C. and everyone else on earth to eat these words later, and many times over.

Plus, where was the girl going with this? She was going, and in a circular way, to the heart of the matter; but she took a few minutes, puffing out the argument with the kind of hortatory flourish they knew so well from the nuns and their tongues, then narrowed it to the case in point and showed cleanly and swiftly that Mary L. Conley, accused, had done nothing but her job of class president. She was not there, never was and never would be there, to answer for her constituency: each had her own will and conscience, not to mention the will and conscience of the single editor, who authored the class testament, toward whom, if the nun chose to redirect her ire, Miss Conley, president, would stand by, because it was, in the end, a mistake, a lapse in taste and—she started raising her voice again—a sign, in any case, of their singular affection for a person they thought good-humored and unpretentious enough to enjoy the joke and therefore, deserving their affection, see the prank in its smallness and irrelevance to the great matters of life and eternity. The nun was hissing now; she was working herself up, and it was clear at this point, from what she was saying, that it was illegal for her, a member of the order F.F.J., to appear in print; it was, in short, a sacrilege; and what was the girl going to do about that?

Mary L. Conley said: if it's any help to you, I resign my position, president of the senior class, editor of the yearbook, and president of the Sodality of Our Lady—is that reparation enough for the indignities done to your name and the name of the Faithful Friends, Mother Transfigurata?

They heard no more; the voices dropped. The next thing that happened was Mary L. Conley issuing out the front door of the school with her lunchbag and schoolbag, with her coat and school shoes— she didn't even take the time to remove the black loafers and store them, safe and unscuffed, in the cloakroom. Miss Kane broke into a run, caught up and stopped the Conley flight. Where you going? Mary L. Conley was crying. She broke away from her friend, Anne Kane, and ran to the bus stop in front of the state offices. Anne Marie Kane watched her: she was wiping her cheeks with her hand and looking up the street; there it was, the Chalkstone bus, and she was on it by the time the recreation bell rang, and the students filed back into the school. There was no Mother T. the whole rest of the day: she must be hiding, someone whispered to Anne Kane in the seventh period, in the nuns' room; and she was. They saw her when the nuns called their cab and all five piled in it, and home.

This was not the only time Mary L. had blown her stack; she was good at it. She wasn't blowing so much now as mouthing off when she needed to, and Uncle Ed, if anyone, was a provocation with his own teasing tongue and air of superiority; Miss Kane herself never invited an explosion: all the years of seeing Mary L. day by day, night by night, she watched her tongue and was more careful now than ever, as Mary L. Conley kept a closer eye on the girl from out of town for a sign of something she didn't like, and wasn't going to swallow.

The summer was hot and it dripped on, day by day; fall was closer and closer and Miss Kane's boyfriend from Minnesota, a future doctor, Dr. Smith, was calling with his plans, now that she was going to be directly across the river, and not way off in the country, and she'd have her own library card and privileges, and not lean on him.

But she did lean on him. She was scared that first night in Crowninshield Hall and decided the best thing was get away as often as possible and hide at the medical school with him, but he didn't like this; it wasn't right; so, when he wanted to be engaged, she—Mrs. Kane told her husband—dumped him, to pay him back. This wasn't correct, Anne Kane told her sister, Ellen, the first time on earth they had a conversation that wasn't all hissing and insults: I just snuck away when I got the chance. Why? What was wrong with him? He was mean. Who was mean? He was. Why? I was there all alone and scared, and he was mean; he wanted to get rid of me. What a jerk. No, he wasn't a jerk; he just—.

Right after Mother Transfigurata and Mary Conley had their blowout, Anne Kane, too, dropped out of Sodality and refused to write for the yearbook. She stayed very near Mary L. Conley at all times, in case anyone tried to get her when she was alone and defenseless. They got to be friends again—Figaro and Mary L.—and Mary told her other friend, Anne Marie Kane, that Mother T., who didn't usually like the Kane girl, too clingy and sugary sweet, had paid her a compliment.

Really? What? What did she say?

She said you were a loyal friend.

She did!

This was the first time Anne Marie Kane got a compliment from the nuns, beside the one of being a lovely girl, which everyone got, and she always remembered it: she was loyal. This was something she was, or at least, *had* been, before she left Providence and her friend Mary L. Conley for good, like a traitor. This was what was wrong, she explained to Ellen Kane, who wanted to know, with people in this new world, what was wrong? They weren't loyal.

Maybe they don't need to be, the sharp-eyed Ellen Kane, fourteen and bound for the public high school, no more uniforms, no more nuns, said.

He needed to be, the sharper-eyed Anne Marie Kane, twenty years old and settled at Harvard, said; and Ellen, her sister, laughed.

I MEET THE FAMILY
AND SHOW MY METTLE

Graceful, he said, like my aunt with the white hair and the
wonderful foot. What? I said. He said it was like a pendulum,
a croquet mallet. My feet were small as raindrops; I pumped
them. Look now, I said.

The aunt's name was Jane: Jane's foot. She had a completely
round, an orbic foot, each toe like a ten-cent rubber ball, veins
like the rivers of the Orient. *Sa tante.*

Dance again, he said. The aunt moved on, her cotton dress
a snowy field of flowers. Big as a bed. The foot was mass, volume,
extension, superfluity and pain. Her form divided the television
screen in two.

Her nature was elastic, her foot controlled. The sewing machine
also had a foot, a flying foot, plus the button attachment. Jane,
Jane. She sat to rest on a brown chair, rocking. Her mouth
opened; I took a cream puff. True, I would never dance as well
as I wished to.

One foot was small, only a black shoe, a stocking and an ankle.
Meek, dormant, mechanical. The mother foot, she said, her face
all red, is automatic, tic-tac. This one, however, she said, pointing
to it, is like a child. At the end of her leg, it was a ham, a tuba.
The foot of his aunt. Am I making a good impression?

You, he said, have the heartless transparency of the normal,
the gigantic ease of movement of a spider on the glass earth.
Therefore, your dancing is fraudulent, tepid. Her foot takes the
eye from beneath the roots, and drags with it a train of memories,
repetition, jaggedness, paradox. Your little feet entrain only the
liquidity of my eyeball. I said—seeing it there, fat as a buddha on
the braided rug—I'm willing to believe you as long as you remain
consistent.

The foot, dearest. The mind. The partners. The nephew was
always demonstrative toward his female relative; I was always
analytic; the aunt had a house of her own. I used to, she said,
share a home with him. She pointed to the nephew as if that were
enough to recall the uncle, who had a bump the size of a transistor
on his head, and a beautiful high tenor voice.

125

Dancing, she said, is the art of the curious. He memorized the steps from the floorplan, R's and L's, dotted lines, crisscrosses, the special foot with its own outline, densely cross-hatched at the vertical axis. What he found out was I was a petty dancer: abbreviated thrusts, short breath, tingly handprints on his back. His aunt danced with the savage foot.

On it was an elastic stocking and a white wool sock. They were forced to stop dancing when the radio announcer came on and that sense of humanity was gone. Their feet.

Dancing is asymmetric, he whispered to me in the back hall, as we listened to the old lady alternating feet to get to the door. It is not, I said loudly. Push and pull, it requires, but eventually both partners will execute about the same number of steps. Asymmetry, I thought, requires mistakes to be made. He shushed me, pointed to the door which opened onto the face of his aunt.

Dancing can take a whole afternoon, even the simplest kind. The music was this and that, thin and fat, violins and woodwinds. He is never asymmetric, I thought, but the minute I stood up and slanted my feet toward him, he backed away, dancing backwards. The aunt looked. Her foot dancing was like a long afternoon, and now this too. She looked at her nephew dancing backwards, and at me; my face was like a simple sandwich. I am almost dead, she thought, and my foot is poison, yet I would rather be dead than be them.

Her nephew sat down on a chair he had backed into and watched too. There was I, light, feet like stars, silent feet. I had no sense of the world under them. I was dancing only with my mind.

Dancing can be impersonal, I thought, only myself on the dance floor. I kept time to the music of the voice of the announcer. My steps were uncomplicated, yet thickly strewn. This is dancing, I told them. I've heard that before, the aunt said.

As we left his ancestral home, the screen door closing behind us, he said gallantly: may I have . . . ? No, I'm better off like this, I said, pivoting, pivoting. I can learn that dance, he said.

HE sat in a small park, all surrounded by buildings, a Harvard park, walled in by the wall. There was inside a cavity, and grief clicking against the sides like a bolt in a vat. Only a minute ago—no, an hour ago, two hours—something had ended, the last thing had fallen out and there was nothing to carry around but this skin, less than a skull, just a cloth really, on a hanger. It was flopped over a stone bench, waiting for the trashmen. It had taken a detour, avoiding the plan to meet David Jacobson, or any other plan. It had made a small jog from the Hall of William James to the park. It was in the park surrounded by bricks and a wall, listening to the traffic, peaceful and empty, a volume of crying, then peaceful and empty. This was a cycle and when it went through a few rounds, it would be over, just a clean skin and a wire hanger.

"In the hall of William James," the sampler wrote on its cloth skin, "a young girl entered dressed like a fool in orange and green, sat down at the oval table under the shiny portraits of famous mugs: William James, Sigmund Freud, Karl Abraham; the dim trio, Harry Stack, Erik E. and Alfred A.; an old friend, the wordy Talcott Parsons; Abraham Maslow, Carl Rogers and B.F. Skinner, and others, framed and in gray suits behind a glass, looking down or away, flanked by more of the same and books of the same, and around this mahogany table, a host of the same, but younger; with a book on the table, a copy by Miss Anne M. Kane, A.B.-elect in Social Relations, of the honors thesis, the wherewithal. They had their thumb on the black book, a story of how a certain culture (because this is what we're talking about: "culture," a difficult word, and used to mean something no one ever forgets) in Northern Europe, fourteenth century: a mess, tense and confused, holy and sick, a harlequinade of foolishness, of loud hungers and fierce punishments, balloons of temptation and teeth-like judgments, fiery cold and fiery heat, letter and spirit; crude offenses to God perfectly matched by worse offenses to the flesh produced (use an arrow here) the Hieronymus Bosch, whose painted men put their heads in an apple and bent their backs so an arrow could plunge in, kissed the princess in a silver bubble and rode a pumpkin to hell; old spindly dogs and blue rocks; a hilarious man, whose comfort was the crayon colors also seen in the St. Joseph Daily Missal, colors loved by Catholics, *in saecula saeculorum.*"

She had looked up. Amen, they should have said. Instead—she would never think about this again, only now in this Gethsemane,

Mass. Avenue—they had shaken out of this black book the ants, rats, snakes, bats of folly: mistakes and carelessness, immaturity and negligence; it was, for these men, a hell hole of impenetralia, rotten with errors surface and deep, with a tendency to make of thin history a fat story, make the story match ("Garden of Earthly Delights") the picture, and not simply find the words for the facts. They had said and she agreed: guilty. Do you, Anne M. Kane? I do, forever and ever. They said it now: amen. Amen, she said, and walked out of the room, remembering the hard judgment the one man had made (see this book? it stinks): no distinction. One week later, he gave her a copy of *his* book: *Life in a Fourteenth Century Village*. "To Anne Kain," they flyleaf said, "with kind regards, Walter Appleton." How come? "Because," he had said, "you and I are interested in the same things."

She would take this book and try to throw it away, but it would never go away. It kept itself there with her as part of the nest of the past, a crown of twigs and apple cores, tacks and grass that fitted so nicely like a brain hat, all plain and sentimental, and there for life.

She was starting to get up from the bench, but no. Here was somebody walking over, David, because he knew this place that she liked to sit in, and could always find her there or in any other place. I'm going to write, she said before he could get one of his words out, the history of the sink. Don't afflict me, he said, sitting next to her on the stone; and it was only then that she noticed he had an affliction. His own book, overworded, thrilling in its speculation on the wonders of the future, thin in fact and systematic thinking, was not a favorite either among the doctors of social science.

A new thing was starting to happen. She could tell as soon as he sat down on the stone and started to speak, then jumped up from the stone, paced around and sat down again. He was talking: he must be talking because his lips were flapping, but she couldn't hear. A nest of thoughts dropped down from the brain to block all the entrances in the head. It was peaceful: the nest itself had its own knots of trouble and was pushing inward, but there was only it, nothing else, and David Jacobson had not even noticed. Nobody could see this, even if they were looking right at her. The enclosure was perfect and perfectly invisible.

❧ The year that was the last year at Harvard was used up by chores and projects, all trivial and none to pierce the soon smooth shell around the head—it was like the head growing another head, an outer head or dry helmet, and a quiet, not unbearable life was found in it. She started, yes, to hear David Jacobson's voice again, while it was still there to be heard: she heard it, there among the other voices and sounds, but not as loud as before, or as full of anger. David Jacobson was one of the angriest boys she had ever met: he had tried to explain to her, starting on the first date, how it was that he came to be the angriest boy at Harvard. It wasn't his fault: he hated Harvard, according to him, and Harvard hated him, according to everyone else. It was a very long story and he told it during that whole time she knew him and they were going together: first, he told it all in one burst over one weekend. The first night, they went out to dinner and walked to Boston and back and sat on the stoop in front of Crowninshield Hall, then snuck into Peabody Terrace and rode the elevator to the top and out to the roof and up a ladder to a higher roof until they were at the highest point at Harvard. He was talking and talked until the sun came up, then down the ladder they came, down the elevator and into the Hayes-Bickford for a greasy breakfast, and back to his room to listen to music—he told her it would take a lifetime for her to hear all the pieces he knew and liked, and he wanted her to hear every one—then, over to Lehman Hall where there was a grand piano and he sat and played Brahms and Schubert—very loud and dramatic; Anne Kane was looking out the window and could see people outside looking up, the playing was so loud and dramatic. He let her go home to change her clothes and he went home to try and sleep, but they met again for a dinner at Winthrop House with all his friends, philosophy and creative writing, film and plexiglas art, essays and Marxism, theater and string quartets, doing imitations of grandmothers and grandfathers speaking a Yiddish English, browbeating, chiding, mocking, feeding and smothering—or, that's how they made it sound, while they drank and ate trays and trays of food and red, orange, and green watery drinks. It was hilarious and there were times she thought she would start laughing again and never stop: these boys were so funny in their imitations and their sweet, serious faces, billowy white shirts and soft-soled shoes; they all looked nervous and tired, trying to do too many things at once and still have a girlfriend, play amateur chamber ensembles, balance a double major, volunteer their time for Phillips Brooks House, work for Allard Loewenstein, write an editorial for the *Crimson* or a poem for the *Advocate,* make weekend excursions to see paintings or lunar eclipses, zoos and arboreta, call home twice a week, bring their shirts to the cleaners, smoke dope and buy

the newest rock 'n roll records, swim in the pool, go to the Brattle
theater, get drunk at a weekly party, play cards in the suite and go to
Symphony Hall rehearsals.

David Jacobson liked these boys and ate dinner with them whenever he had time—having a girlfriend up at the Cliff took up weekends and some weeknights because he had to spend time with her,
too, and he had always had a girlfriend: the minute he arrived at
Harvard, he plugged his phone in, flipped through the Radcliffe Reg-
ister and called ten girls, and only the girls whose names he recognized: daughter of the editor of the *New York Times* was one, he told
little Anne Kane, girlfriend number fifteen, and very late in the season; daughter of the richest man in Connecticut, daughter of a famous Broadway musical team, half of whose name was borrowed
from the lyricist, the other half from the composer; daughter of the
American ambassador to France, daughter of a TV talk-show host
broadcasting coast to coast, who had brought with her to
Cambridge two baby cheetahs, until they forced her to send them
back to where she got them and she went, too, shortly after. There
were others, all famous, all beautiful, all rich, and all snooty, and
not a single one, David Jacobson said half in a rage, but better controlled now, would go out on a date with him. He said once he
thought it might be because he was Jewish; Annie Kane didn't know
what it was because David Horace Mann Jacobson was the most interesting boy on earth and although she couldn't account for the
blindness of these famous daughters, never as long as she lived would
she understand what someone like this—so smart, so vocal, so talented in every way: art (his paintings were on the walls), photogra-
phy (he gave a slide show for her and two of his Cliffie friends, just
friends, although they adored him and were staying close by to be
next in line), drama (he had directed his high school annual play, but
this was something so important he put off telling her the full story
for weeks, then told it in five hours flat, with no digressions or extra
details), music (piano, voice and conducting, summers at Inter-
lochen, plus 1,000,000 talented musical girlfriends), science (pre-
med and doing everything in half the time with no F's or I's), mime
(he had entertained thousands of black children on the streets of Chicago in his mime suit), chess (he was going to Providence just to beat
her Uncle Ed, who, Annie Kane had mentioned, was pretty good at
chess), languages (sometimes he spoke nothing but French in restaurants and on the street; Annie Kane could speak French, too, but not
that well; he forced her to talk: "Don't be such an egotist," he told

her, "keep talking until you get it; that's what I do."), math (perfect scores on the SAT's—he must have said this a million times, but no matter how many times he said it, she still believed him), would see in someone like her. What did, she wondered, he need (he wondered this, too) Harvard for? Harvard needed him: he didn't have to tell her this, she always knew it. The problem was it didn't matter how much David H. M. brought to Harvard, no matter how many things he brought . . . sometimes he reminded Annie, when she still had a sense of humor but those days were long past, of the banana man on Captain Kangaroo with the things he could pull out of his head, out of his past and out of his pocket.

His pocket was a marvel, too. His dad, Dr. Jacobson, a woman doctor—babies and female complaints; what in Providence they called "women's troubles" but what was, in these circles, OB/GYN, sat down at his desk in Chicago twice a year, at the beginning of each semester and uncapped his pen—a nice pen, Mont Blanc was its name, very black and fat with a gold tip—and opened his check-book (D.H.M.J. had told A. many times about this scene and A. loved hearing about it. A. loved any story about the doctor, his father, and his many interesting ways.), a checkbook as big as a geography book with rows and stacks of checks and a lovely picture of downtown Chicago on each one; he got himself comfortable (he was a very methodical man) and asked David in a quiet voice exactly how much money he would need to complete his semester; David Jacobson would pass a sheet of loose-leaf paper to the doctor with his tuition, his room and board, his book budget, his record budget, his dining-out budget, his plane tickets, his lab fees, his symphony tickets, his Boston Celebrity Series tickets, his club dues, his psychiatrist bills, his rented furniture bill, and a thousand other incidentals A. couldn't keep track of: it was a more complicated life than she was used to. Dr. Jacobson would scan this list with his careful eyes and when he was finished, glance over at David, standing next to him. Is this all? he would say. Then—and this was the exciting part—the tired but tireless, quiet but powerful, methodical but fearless, overworked but feisty, skinny but muscular, exacting but generous, abrupt but loving, taciturn yet adoring father of David would lick the tip of his pen (Really? And he's a doctor?), rest his arm precisely on the glass-topped table and etch out the name of his son in full: Mr. David Horace Mann Jacobson, and then where it said Pay To The Order Exactly, he would add an extra 1,000 to whatever exhaustive figure David Jacobson had so meticulously worked up.

It took a long time, this process, but it was always worth it and the pocket of David Jacobson was a bottomless well of dinners, tickets, presents, long-distance phone calls, records, bicycles, art supplies, treats, and comforts.

❧ Whatever happened to David What's-his-name, that weird boy you knew, remember him? you know who I mean, people still asked her because David Jacobson was not the run-of-the-mill boyfriend, even to people here. He was different, he stood out, even in a place where everyone stood out. People weren't noticing just how far he stood out, true; they weren't giving him the benefit of that kind of notice, but they *had* noticed it; everyone noticed how different he was. Most people didn't like the difference, maybe that was it. Someone had suggested this, but Anne Kane dismissed it as improbable; if people picked this place and this place picked them because they were a fraction of what David Jacobson was, then why wouldn't they give David Jacobson the credit for being all that and more so? Why? They were jealous, that's why. So, little by little, because he wasn't getting from people even what he had gotten in his township high school—and even that wasn't so very much because he wasn't popular, just admired because he was talented in everything—he stopped doing all the things he *could* do: he put his slide show away and never took another picture; he let his oils and acrylics get all dried up, then threw them out, although he kept his paintings: he sent them all home in a big flat box addressed to his father; he stopped trying out for plays at the Loeb and plays in the houses, when no one would pick him for anything; he told his father no, he didn't want to rent a piano, and no, he didn't want the baby grand shipped from Chicago; he never went to Providence to beat Uncle Ed at chess; he never put his mime suit on, not even just so Annie Kane could see him and enjoy his fun; he stopped speaking French like a native and put a letter in the mail to a film school, then wrote a lot of famous directors, telling them of his plans and schemes. This was something completely new he had never done before, and the only way to do it was to leave Harvard and do it somewhere else, which is what he did. *That's* where David Jacobson is. Where? In Hollywood. Get out. It's true. He's trying to make films. First, he'll try an underground film, then a few cartoons, then no one will hear from him while he writes what he's always wanted to write (What?). A screenplay about the 60s (Really?). Yes, then he'll be back, Miss Kane had told Mary Conley, who came to Cambridge that one time

132

and met David Jacobson, listened to his records, went up the ladder at Peabody, heard a couple of long stories, and did some other things.

What Mary Conley thought of David Jacobson, though, Annie Kane would never know because Mary Conley didn't want her to know. She let herself be talked into staying for the weekend; she smoked some grass, she slept on the extra bed, like Emily Goldstein did, with David Jacobson and Annie Kane. She did all this and seemed to like it, but when Annie Kane asked her a few weeks later what she thought of David Jacobson, Mary L. Conley said: Don't ask me that. Why? Just don't ask me. I like him; leave it at that. He's different; he's interesting. I've never met anyone like him. "You think," Miss Kane asked her friend, "I should stay with him?" I'm not saying that; I don't know what you should do.

A week or two later, when they were talking on the phone, and David was getting ready to leave without even graduating, Mary L. said: You'll never guess who wrote me a twelve-page letter. Who? Guess. I can't guess: who? Your friend, David.

Mary L. was invited for another visit, right before the end. David Jacobson seemed very eager to see her, but this time she didn't come. I can't. Why? I've busy with my own life, Anne Mary. I can't get myself all involved with your life; I'm not up to it. I don't even understand it. What don't you understand? I don't know; if I were in your place, I wouldn't know what to do, that's all. You mean—with him? I mean all of it.

Not that long after, David Jacobson went away forever. Anne Kane missed him. There was nobody on earth like David Jacobson, nobody. The world was empty without him and his ways. Now she was alone. At first, it was painful every minute, then it just felt dull and ordinary. Plus, there were other problems. There was the book. The book was still there, filed in among the other delusions, and bigger than before.

A certain pattern the days had now. In the room the school had given to her just for being a student, nothing more, and would take away on no account, was housed the derided and faulty book with all its mystery; namely, what it had committed for its crime, or what crime had been placed in it, and who had put it there. There were days in the sweet silence of the room, a room with a window, when the book too, all black and white, was steeped in its own silence, taking a bath of dust on the floor, secret and closed, dull in its muteness. Other days, it whisked around and battered at things; it produced in its author's brain replicas of its artist's hellscapes. Still other days, it rose in calm judgment; the crimes of its author were fruitful and multiplied in the shame of having made it and put it up as a front, so poor, ignorant and obvious. Other times, it was a helpless black rag. Sometimes she put it in the bed, after she threw the bed away and left just the thin mattress on the floor, eye-level with the floor and its book. Although she did not consult its inner sheets, the book in all its ugliness of mistakes, became a friend and a twin.

First, she put up a fool's struggle to keep the Harvard Library from getting it back and putting it and its dirt on a dry shelf among the other infant books. They would not get this black book or any copy of it. Wrong. They owned it; it was the thing they got; she got the paper degree only if they got the inferior book to ridicule forever, with its new title page: No Distinction. There was no way to fight them; they got the one that lived on the floor of the room; she got the copy, a group of sheets with no black binder, just an elastic to hold it all in. It was not the same book, naked without its widow's weeds; so she took it home to Providence and put it down in the cellar so it could replace its black coat with a new coat of mildew and rust. It grew a set of chancres, too, and the paper curled and started to smell different. It grew its own kind of life down there, and let it.

❧ The winter was gone, and a tender spring. These years were almost over: it was nearly time to get married. But first, to move out of the dwelling; the dwelling emptied itself of the author when the library got its book. It wasn't cruel, didn't spit the author into the street; emptied, rather, the occupant, disguised in a black robe, like the book, at the end of a graduation parade and into the graduation tent. The Kanes were there, the sun was blinding and the city and tent heaved in a summery heat. The young doctors issued their formal invitation to the occupant, not yet in the street, to join them and follow their silver sled home.

But the house of the head, imitating its book, was now faulty, and all the Eagles in the world couldn't repair its faults because no one knew about the cap of solitude and the things that had fallen out of it when it broke; no one knew what parts had gone, or what was there before—an inventory had never been taken. Faults moved to the surface, forming a skin or coat of panic buttons which, if they weren't pressed by a friendly hand, pressed themselves. The occupant was forced to narrow her circle, to close up her hours: there was no brain shell, so the world needed to be a fence or walled enclosure.

Moved very slowly in their paper slippers and talked very slowly. The occupant slid in a slow and careful way to the armored car of Mary Mallon, social worker, and was driven in the cold and perfect car to the HCMHC, every day and at the same time. They would hop out of the car, Mary Mallon on her spindly legs and tiny boots and Miss A. Kane, with the weight all in her feet. Inside was the heat of the building and the patients waiting. Barry at the door: Hi Miss Mallon, hi Miss, hi Miss, and Mrs. McDonald, the receptionist, already with a smile on her face and a good word: no matter how early they arrived, Mrs. McDonald, whose ailing husband would be propped up at home in his mechanical bed with medicines and a lunch bag, a thermos of juice, books, magazines, a couple of pads to doodle on, the cards he received yesterday, if he received any—she had explained her routine to A. Kane—and the remote control unit to the new color TV Mrs. McDonald was spending the rest of her life, she said, trying to pay for, in his lap; with little Janie, Arthur, Mary Lou and Candace packed up and off to school (her sister-in-law would run across the street to make their lunch and see that they ate it and didn't pester their father too much, and the father hadn't fallen out of bed and have to call the brother Lou to haul him up, 300 pounds and inert) was already there with a circle of patients drinking their coffee in the vicinity of her desk and chair. They look like they're at a cocktail party, A. Kane had said once, but Miss Mallon didn't find remarks like that particularly funny, especially when they were told at the expense of the mentally disabled, who couldn't defend themselves and wouldn't even get the joke if they had the benefit of hearing it.

By now, the familiar patients were back on the street. Ginny Cooper was in high school and they hadn't heard any reports good or bad, although it wasn't a good sign that she wasn't showing up for day care sessions either after school or on Saturday mornings, the shrewd Mrs. Peters said, and she could predict as well as any what would happen next. They were only good for so long—Miss Kane had made this observation: a stay in the center gave them a few months of normalcy or what was normal in Haverhill, and then back they came, all fallen apart again, everything about them would look different: they were fatter or much thinner, none of their clothes would match and what they had on would be grimy and wrinkled; their eyes would be a different color, darker and muddy or much lighter and glossy-looking; faces were puffy and shapeless or thin with the skin pulled tight and the eyes popped. In they came when their weeks or months were up, and back they went to the beginning: lying in the ward and shuffling down to swear and rave in group until their drugs quieted them and finally brought them peace; then they would enter a low period full of despair and silence and finally, grim and practical with a list of things to do and not to do, the family would arrive in the beachwagon or the old jalopy and the patient would go, be driven home to the awkward and delicate course of days and nights.

Barry was still there (hi there, Barry), but Joey Mahan, poor Joey, was sent to the state institution: he was not able, it was the decision of the staff and his doctor, to handle the routine and freedom of a mental health center and needed greater vigilance and structure: these were the words they used. What it meant was they couldn't send him home anymore; the family was barely managing with the disabled child and so little money and the wife, after a bout of hepatitis and in that awful winter when it snowed from November to March and unemployment in the city rose to 25 percent to include poor Mrs. Mahan, who had had a good paying job in a suit factory, now working a counter part-time at the Four Aces Dry Cleaners on Main, right on the spot—someone remarked and tears came to the eyes of A. Kane, who never cried or only cried once a year if she really had to, when she heard it—where the old L.B. and E.E. Bloom's used to be, remember Bloom's? They built a cleaners and a carwash there.

Marie Battiste, like Ginny, was still home but she'd be back too, unannounced, in the middle of the night and probably brought in by ambulance as she started to tear the house apart or went for her husband with a golfclub or a carving knife. Eddie Foley, another familiar face, was dead and nobody knew quite how. The family was not communicating with the center, what family there was—just an older sister, Mrs. Peters had said, and some aunts and uncles. Someone read about it in the paper and he wasn't even supposed to have had grounds privileges. He was on the ward a couple of days and then vanished. None of his therapists or guardians knew where he was.

A. Kane made a trip to one of the resident psychiatrists right after Eddie died. He told her she wasn't making a clear distinction between herself and the patients, addicted, poor, drunk, withered and crazy, a difference between them, might as well be dead as live the way they did, all shut in, or on the streets of this old mill town; and herself, fresh from a snooty Ivy League school. He was right, but she had made some of these connections on her own. And, there *were* connections. The knowledge in the book, No Distinction, so cracked and stupid, was useful here because the patients liked to paint pictures of themselves. Marie Battiste drew faces that were all eyes, each eye with a double set of eyelashes, carefully drawn, like teeth; and Ginny Cooper, whose tremulous hands had been trying for a perfect likeness of the faces in *Time* magazine, had asked the old Miss Kane, trainee, to help her do it. I have, she told the nice doctor who had interviewed her for the job, the experience necessary to talk to these patients, and now it was true.

Things were working out and she had a guardian Mary who would protect her from excursions in pride or empty accomplishments. Miss M. had already delivered in the wonderful car some excellent corrections and curbs—like she did to the patients— advising the bag of faults liquefied on the seat beside her not to deploy her arty and showboat terms in a place where the patients could hear because they didn't know what these terms meant so what good were they? Plus, it could hurt their feelings, drive them deeper into insanity, maybe kill them. The occupant, so sleek and lifeless, but so useful, knew—if knowledge is more than a scratch or petty opening onto the skin—that Miss M. didn't know what the words meant either, that they would draw her deeper into insanity, maybe kill—. For a while, this knowledge was inert among the other brain junk, then it began to come out, sometimes in the form of a joke or a funny word in the wrong place. The things that were on the inside all these years were starting to come out. She could feel them coming.

And things were beginning to slow down, the toil of it. She was getting married. Who? The early life, Christ College, with its simple round of classes, chattering, and dances, and the single pains of March and Michael Fury, was bearing its perfect fruit, Mr. Frazier; this fruit had fallen off early and rolled to another tree, then rolled back and settled in a room, dark and warm, played the guitar and sometimes sang. She had not, A.K., identified herself yet to Mr. Frazier as a patient in a helmet with a black book, one whose hectic lives had collapsed into the simple line the green car followed to Haverhill and back, and again and back, with the young doctors to handle her at home, if any probs should come up. She explained nothing.

Instead, she arranged to meet him, tracking him down to the far-away tree and bringing him back to within a mile of the doctors' flat, and fresh himself from two years on a submarine deep under the ocean, all encased like A.K. in a metal cap and by himself. She called him up on the telephone and he came to the doctors' house while she was on the bathroom floor washing it in a hurry because they all had chores to do and better do them or else. So kind and quiet he was; they walked the length from Brookline to Boston and over the bridge to Cambridge, a steady pacing, and he was willing to visit all her remembered spots: the Parrot, the Pewter, the Hayes, and skirt around the other things. They did it a few more times and decided to get married—and what does he do? First, he went into a submarine, underwater all those years, like me—and form a strong alliance, him and me, against the falseness of the world because, he knew this, you can evade the world, all those long months under the water, making a slow path in the middle layers of the water. You can have a life, completely your own, separate from all that. All what? Everything else, including a string of things from the Kanes to the doctors, even including, she could see, Mary L. Conley, and her related strings. Under the water was just the smooth water and private thoughts left uninterrupted.

The Kanes, meanwhile, were planning a wedding. A cake was ordered, white with white frosting, white frosting roses and little silver bullets: it had no words written on it, just a flat, one-layer square on a paper doily. The sandwiches, chicken and beef, were made and frozen in somebody's refrigerator, and the necessary battles had been fought about the costume of the bride, who settled for a flesh-colored suit to cover the emaciated form, thinned out from work and nightmares. Presents of an assortment were arrayed on a metal table covered with a cloth: toaster-oven, glass candlesticks, pale blanket, sugar bowl and pitcher in pewter, nothing silver for a wedding this fast—a sailor and almost flunked out of Harvard.

And the Holy Savior Church was the setting for the marriage, and back they went to Boston. A quiet like a dark wave continued to form itself around the couple, Kenmore Square, and all memories fell under it as it coursed over its own space of painful and delicate years and hours. In those years, and in an hour, Anna dropped into the subway hole and made the first getaway.

THE BEATING

They were all bad boys, stinking and rotten. They gave their mother, Malkrot, their worst, but she wasn't worth more. They bombed the house, a garbage, with clams and dirt, with wet gum and milkpods, they showed the girls the cut in their back and stuck out their tongue at Jesus in his pale suit on the altar until their eyeballs were strained at the root. They did all this and they did more.

I was at that time in my right mind, ten, ten and a half, a crybaby. I ached in my joints from blasts of growth, my skin was roiling and pilling in attempts to mate, as if mate meant remove the skin like a thin coat and assume a second coat. Apply to yourself a dot of Lepage gum glue and roll in an angora sweater, fix the twelve lime lollipops to hairs and soles of the feet and depend like Simon Peter until the thought balls empty out and zero around on the floor like those old black pennies and Spanish cooties.

Here was where I was, a canker, and yet a drift of blue, a bottle skating down the parkway and living just to fall down the sewer. There were things waiting for me: belts, tire irons, snowballs with surprises, pins and needles, pliers, dirt cookies, hot balls, things in the face and around the rim of the body.

And now I'm what they call a full twit, a finished, and you've never heard me talk so brave. But I've cooked and spoiled, I've wrent the old skin and spilled my emptiness all over and through, and still more. You'll want to hear how.

The soil falls lightly on the ground. I skid around on it. The two I mentioned have prepared my way and my neck stoops all the way for them to have their way with the ball, my head. If you give the boys the means to pain, they'll take and give it back to you, licked clean and there you're ahead and back at the beginning again. They give me a small boot, I give them a milky cry, a groan. I pill my heart and liver and speak ribbons of tongue, give forth the unction of my inner, a soul like a plastic shoe, baby shoe all blue. My pockets.

All ready and ready to deal with the further pain, the future foot.

The boys: Oggie and Spackle. How they prepared me. Late one day, an ordinary, I spun out of my crisp with a flat hat, a large but dwindling dress, my flat but fortunate figure flicking its parts and points down the street of my home, a tenement. Down the street where there were two: O and S, waiting. Waiting, they gambled on time and freedom and the cotton ball that was my brain and tricked me down on the ground, spooled my outer trim and welded my parts in a fan-tide of spigot and clamp. I was there and they. I twisted my wreck off the sidewalk floor and cried into my shirt or vest, my hold-up, the things that were still around me and the part of my blooded tongue that was still sticking there to the sidewalk and a little stream of ants, their own family and ideas.

(I'm just getting started.)

Too late. My words were poor: I had no words, but they were poor and the weak smile on my face. My lady mother came up to me and said. I was full of my own awareness and the secret wormhole that was my life with an egg settling in it and the old cracked bones, the threads that went with it and a small brain pan, thin in its holding. You will, she said, but it was already and the silence came and roosted on us, its fat legs and trim feet.

Remember, mote, that thou art dust, I told everyone I met and they were grateful for the reminder and gave me a return. Return this, they said, to her and things would spin and wave, a trumpet come up to my ear and blast, and my body, a loaded skin, shaken by its reedy neck. Even the wretched like to feel thinly sainted, a good gob, true to themselves in their rounded heels, shoes bumped up against shoes. My boys, the two, roamed the necks and parts of the neighborhood combing for the thing they loved to press and poke, pill and test for softness. I could hear them, although I was in my chalice, speaking praises and enjoying the afternoon caress of the airs, though wished, as usual, to give of myself, to fold a big batter, present and unfold. This was the art of it.

Down the street circling a garbage they were. In my ear and out of my ear the brine of my mother's midday verbal cramp, letter to a churl. I combed through my sentiments and hung a lively curtain in front of my face, dabbling in nothing while she prosed of the hard grains in my soul and my flesh with its stance of re- pulsiveness and dégout. O.K. for now, I said, and set my flame of life on low or empty. Returned for this quantity of prose, a certain gassy prose of my own: a series of commandments to myself, and then heard in the recess of the home this message: hey lay off the kid will you. This slow bullet through the verbiage of charge and counter-command gave me the idea: captivate your audience with the thing you bring from the bottom, the wonderful undersized nits and mauves, the cones of logic and grim earrings of life as we knew, flesh poked with rememberings, acid coats and shriveling balloons, a note of praise for the things you could collect in your tongue.

And out, to be whacked until finally (here's where it happens) I brought my spine-like fist out of its pocket of fleece. What kind of thing? The four eyes of Oggie and Spackle circled the thing and made a melted sound with their lips and teeth. The pretense of it, the foolery and they brought their eyes closer: I turned it up, the fist, so they could see the underside; I showed them its relation to the past, to history, to the whiteness of the neighborhood and the new hoods on the saints in the church, all lowing in a quiet voice, Lenten manner. See this, I said, mentioning the names of their mothers and the rocks that could fly in the night, the sizzling steaks slipping right out of the pans, the endless fiery stream of cutting words into the cloud of the skull. I was preaching the mountain, returning the unlacerated cheek and tiny foot in a Maryjane or an old stale sneaker, and they were gaping. I filled their gape with temps, reminding this sullen flock of the shortness of life, of the dark spaces, of the dry thin surface of the globe and the dancing hairs of life that could be theirs if they would settle an inheritance of goodwill on the girlish body and its integrity. But, by then, taking out the spoons, rakes, picture cards, animal feet, folded up papers, bottle caps, shreds and fines of things from the outside pockets and tricking me, giving me of the fruits of the earth, tarnishing the heavy pulp of my face, its soul, with goods. And then, behind that, standing, as my little stick arms reached, the bloody spins and negative scrapings, the fingers and satellites, the nearness, and infiltering of all the parts and points and the beginning, and to begin, and finally.

Still spilling from the lassitude of my mouth, a limp curl of prose, a pale cycle of imaginings, a loop, and onto the sidewalk, a ringworm. They watched it. Until it drove up, the car, and I was shoveled onto the seat and driven up to here, as age drives us up to here and leaves the worm and blood of the past, Oggie and Spackle, this and that, all dry and flecked, soon to be gone.

Other Books in the Series

THE VERY RICH HOURS

Designed by Chris L. Smith
Composed by Brushwood Graphics, Inc., in Sabon text and display
Printed and bound by the Maple Press Company
in Holliston's Kingston Natural and
Lindenmeyr's Elephant Hide and stamped in gold.